WHO'S WHO?

Elizabeth looked at Jessica's expression in the mirror. Her sister had a look on her face that could only be descirbed as scheming.

"What?" Elizabeth asked, growing suspicious. "What is it?"

"I figured out what to do about tonight," Jessica told her.

"That's good," Elizabeth replied. "What are you going to do?" she asked after a pause.

"You mean, what are *we* going to do," Jessica corrected her.

Elizabeth whirled around to face her twin. "What are you talking about?" Her heart began pounding rapidly.

Jessica walked over and stood next to Elizabeth. Their identical images looked back at them from the mirror. "We've done it before," Jessica said softly.

"Oh no, you don't! I'm not getting involved in one of your twisted plots."

Jessica lifted her chin stubbornly. "Didn't you say you owed me one?"

Elizabeth looked down at her new dress and then closed her eyes. She was doomed.

SWEET VALLEY HIGH

WHO'S WHO

Written by
Kate Williams

Created by
FRANCINE PASCAL

BANTAM BOOKS
NEW YORK · TORONTO · LONDON · SYDNEY · AUCKLAND

RL 6, IL age 12 and up

WHO'S WHO
A Bantam Book / February 1990

Sweet Valley High is a registered trademark of Francine Pascal.

Conceived by Francine Pascal

Produced by Daniel Weiss Associates, Inc.
33 West 17th Street
New York, NY 10011

Cover art by James Mathewuse

ISBN 0-553-28352-9

Published simultaneously in the United States and Canada

Bantam Books are published by Bantam Books, a division of Bantam Doubleday Dell Publishing Group, Inc. Its trademark, consisting of the words "Bantam Books" and the portrayal of a rooster, is Registered in U.S. Patent and Trademark Office and in other countries. Marca Registrada. Bantam Books, 666 Fifth Avenue, New York, New York 10103.

PRINTED IN THE UNITED STATES OF AMERICA

OPM   0 9 8 7 6 5 4 3 2 1

WHO'S WHO

One

"I'm telling you, Liz. The boys around here are so immature it makes me want to join a convent sometimes."

Elizabeth Wakefield grinned. Her identical twin sister, Jessica, was always complaining about how pathetically unsophisticated the boys at Sweet Valley High were. In spite of how she felt, however, Jessica had dated nearly all of them, and now she had finally run out of guys to go out with.

"The junior and senior boys would have to proclaim a national day of mourning if you did that," Elizabeth teased. She struggled to zip up the dress she was trying on. "Hey, can you help me with this?"

She unlatched the dressing room door to let

her sister in. Jessica heaved a world-weary sigh and joined Elizabeth in the cramped space.

When Elizabeth turned back to the mirror, she saw the reflections of two quintessential California girls, each with sun-kissed blond hair, delicate oval faces, eyes the blue-green of the Pacific Ocean, and perfect size-six figures. Each girl wore a gold lavaliere, a sixteenth birthday present from their parents. Down to the dimple in each girl's left cheek, Elizabeth and Jessica were absolutely identical.

They were only carbon copies on the outside, however. Their personalities were as different as rock is to classical music. Elizabeth was the thoughtful one, the one people turned to when they had problems. She longed to be a professional writer some day, so she devoted a lot of time to writing articles, as well as a column in *The Oracle*, Sweet Valley High's newspaper. She could always be counted on to head a committee or to step in at the last minute if someone else didn't follow through. Elizabeth had a steady boyfriend, Todd Wilkins, with whom she spent much of her free time. Although she had many friends and was one of the most popular girls at Sweet Valley High, there was only one person, other than her twin, with whom she shared her innermost secrets, and that was her best friend, Enid Rollins.

Elizabeth's twin sister, Jessica, was also one of the most popular girls at Sweet Valley High, although for very different reasons. While Elizabeth was calm and quiet, Jessica was outgoing and exuberant. Being cocaptain of the varsity cheerleading squad was just one way for Jessica to be in her favorite place: the spotlight. Her enthusiasm was contagious, and people liked being around her, so she was usually surrounded by a group of friends. She raced along in high gear, changing boyfriends, hobbies, and philosophies of life from one day to the next. She was excitement and adventure in a five foot six inch frame.

Yet, in spite of their differences, Elizabeth and Jessica shared an almost magical bond that no one else could understand. They could sometimes finish each other's sentences, and each twin always knew when her sister was worried or sad or in trouble. Even though their separate friends and different activities often kept them apart, at the end of the day, Elizabeth had Jessica and Jessica had Elizabeth.

"So what do you think of this dress?" Elizabeth asked her twin. "You don't think it's too wild for me, do you?"

Jessica frowned and gave Elizabeth's image in the mirror a critical once-over. "No, not at all. It's perfect for you."

Elizabeth sighed. "I know."

The strapless dress was made of a shimmery fabric that looked blue from one angle and green from another. The annual Valentine Day's dance was coming up at school, and Elizabeth had decided it was time for a new dress. The moment she had seen this one she had fallen in love with it.

"But it's way over my budget," she said. Shaking her head, she began unzipping it. "I really can't afford it."

Jessica's jaw dropped. "What's the problem? Just charge it on Mom's account. You can worry about paying for it *after* you have it. Mom won't mind when she sees how great you look in it."

"That's the way *you* would do it," Elizabeth said, smiling. "Not me."

Jessica shook her head in disgust. "Elizabeth Wakefield, if you spend your whole life being so principled, you'll never have any fun."

Elizabeth laughed and put her jeans and pink cotton sweater back on. With a twinge of regret, she left the blue-green dress hanging on the rack outside the dressing room. She gave the sale dresses at Lisette's another quick survey, but there wasn't anything she liked even half as much.

"I give up," she said. "Let's just go."

Soon the twins were strolling through the center atrium of the Valley Mall. It was just after five o'clock on Wednesday, and the mall was filling up with after-work shoppers.

"Hey, look at that!" Jessica said suddenly.

Elizabeth looked where her sister was pointing. A new business had just opened. The sign over the door read, Lovestruck Computer Dating and a smaller sign in the window announced Teens Our Specialty.

Jessica was looking at Elizabeth with a hopeful, eager expression in her eyes.

"Oh, no, you don't, Jessica!" Elizabeth warned. "You know what happened last time you tried that—you fixed Steve up with Miss Fright Night, and *you* got that guy who wanted to be an undertaker!"

Jessica gave her twin a look of weary patience. "Liz, that was the wrong kind of service. It didn't attract the right types. Look at that sign—it says they specialize in teenagers."

Elizabeth was skeptical. Months ago, Jessica had worked part-time at Perfect Match, another dating service. At the time, their older brother, Steven, had just lost his girlfriend to leukemia. Naturally, the matchmaker in Jessica went to work with the files in the office. But the perfect matches she found for Steven were not so perfect at all, and the boy Jessica decided on for herself had positively ghoulish ambitions! Jessica had spent a whole party just trying to avoid him. After all, who wanted to hear about the history of embalming? Not Jessica, that was for sure.

"Come on," Jessica said airily, leading the way. "I have to check this out. This Valentine's Day I plan to be in love." Blond hair swishing around her shoulders, Jessica strode ahead.

Elizabeth stayed put for a moment. Her twin's supreme confidence in spite of past disasters never failed to amaze her. But that was one of the things Elizabeth loved most about Jessica. With a smile, Elizabeth followed her twin into the store.

"Each applicant fills out one of these questionnaires," the red-haired receptionist was telling Jessica. "Then it goes into the computer, and you get matched up. It's very scientific. And as a special promotion, we're only charging five dollars per application."

Jessica was nodding agreeably, but there was a gleam in her eyes that Elizabeth knew well. It was a speculative, scheming look that meant Jessica was cooking up a plan.

"My sister needs a questionnaire, too," Jessica told the receptionist.

Elizabeth blinked. "What—?"

"Come on, Liz," Jessica broke in, steering her away from the counter. She had two questionnaires in her hand. "Just hush for a second."

They sat down at a little table in an area that was screened off for privacy.

"Jessica, you know I'm not going to—"

"It's not really for you, Liz. Don't worry," Jessica whispered. She arranged both of the questionnaires in front of her and selected a pencil from the ones on the table. "I've got an idea."

Elizabeth sat back in her chair and regarded her sister warily. "Jessica," she began slowly, "why do I get the feeling I don't want to know what you're doing?"

"Relax, Liz." Jessica tapped the eraser end of her pencil on the table and gave Elizabeth a mischievous grin. "I have it all figured out. Last time, I answered all the questions correctly— you know, my hobbies and interests, what kind of music I like. Stuff like that."

"Isn't that the way you're supposed to do it?" Elizabeth asked.

Jessica waved her hand dismissively. "Only if you want the same old type of guy you've always dated."

Elizabeth grinned. There wasn't one type of

guy Jessica had always dated: she had dated so many boys that they couldn't possibly fit into a single category. But Elizabeth didn't think it was worth mentioning that fact. When Jessica had a plan, nothing could change her mind.

"See, what I'll do now is fill out *two* forms with different names," Jessica explained. "Then I'll put different answers on each. That way I'll get a better range of responses. Isn't that brilliant?"

Elizabeth groaned and shook her head. "Brilliant, Jess. Just brilliant."

"I knew you'd think so," Jessica said cheerfully. She bit her lip in concentration. "Let me think. . . ."

In a burst of energy, Jessica began filling out the first form. In a few minutes she was finished with that one and started on the second. Elizabeth pulled the first sheet toward her and read through it.

"Daniella Fromage" seemed to be an intellectual. She liked foreign films, modern poetry, French cuisine, and world travel. Her idea of a perfect evening was "a meaningful conversation in front of a crackling fire, with an opera on the stereo."

Elizabeth tried not to laugh. "Jess, first of all, isn't this name a bit, uh, bizarre?"

"What do you mean? It's perfect," Jessica said absently, still busily scribbling away on the second form.

Shaking her head, Elizabeth put down the first questionnaire and attempted to read the next one upside down. She squinted, trying to make out the name.

"*Magenta Galaxy?*" Elizabeth put one hand over her mouth to keep from giggling. Sometimes her twin got pretty strange ideas.

"Isn't it a cool name?" Jessica said. She grinned as she turned the form around for Elizabeth to read.

"Magenta" was a wild rocker whose passions were "everything new and anything hot." She liked fast cars, loud dance bands, the latest fashions—the wilder the better. Her perfect evening consisted of cruising the hippest music clubs in L.A. and ending up in a coffee shop at four in the morning, eating hamburgers and dancing on the countertop.

Jessica was smiling gleefully while Elizabeth read. "Isn't it perfect? I couldn't decide if I wanted a really sophisticated, cultured guy or a wild, daring type. This way I'll get both!"

"I don't know what you'll get with these, but you'll definitely get something," Elizabeth said. She met her sister's eyes. "Are you positive this is a good idea?"

Jessica put on a look of injured innocence. "What could go wrong, Liz? I think it's a great idea."

"But it never works when you try to be someone you're not," Elizabeth said in a concerned voice. "Remember how you acted when you first met A.J.?"

A flicker of unhappiness crossed Jessica's face. A. J. Morgan was the one boy Jessica had had a serious relationship with. When he first moved to Sweet Valley, Jessica fell for him hard. But at the same time she got the crazy idea that he liked serious, thoughtful, quiet girls, girls like Elizabeth. So Jessica spent her first two weeks with A. J. living a masquerade, trying to change her personality to please him. Luckily, when Jessica finally showed her true colors he had liked her even more, so it all worked out. After a couple of months, however, Jessica realized she wasn't cut out for a steady relationship. Even so, breaking up with A. J. had been one of the saddest times of her life.

"That was completely different," Jessica decided after a moment.

Elizabeth didn't see how it was different. *Either you're honest and act like yourself or you don't*, she thought.

"Hey, listen," Jessica went on, lowering her

10

voice a notch. "Don't these personalities sound familiar to you?" She eyed Elizabeth with an impish grin.

Elizabeth scanned the questionnaires again. "Well, I don't know. Were you thinking of anyone in particular?"

"Of course!" Jessica crowed. "Can't you guess?"

Daniella Fromage, the cultured sophisticate, loved classical music, poetry. Elizabeth frowned. "Now that you mention it, this sounds sort of like Suzanne Hanlon."

"Exactly! And I was thinking of Dana Larson for Magenta Galaxy," Jessica said.

Suzanne and Dana both attended Sweet Valley High. In Elizabeth's opinion, Jessica couldn't have picked two personalities that differed more.

"Then why don't you just use their correct names, give their real addresses and phone numbers, and forget about your crazy plan?" Elizabeth suggested.

Jessica frowned. "No way. The thing is, we have to make sure Mom and Dad don't answer the phone when I start getting calls for Magenta and Daniella. Say you'll go along with it, Liz. Please?" She gave Elizabeth a pleading look.

"Jessica!" Elizabeth covered her face with her hands. "This is *crazy!*"

"But you'll go along with it, right?" Jessica urged.

Elizabeth raised her eyes and looked at her twin. Jessica was the hardest person in the world to say no to.

"OK," she agreed. "I'll go along with it."

Fortunately, the receptionist was talking on the phone when Elizabeth and Jessica returned to the desk. Jessica dropped ten dollars on the desk, then slipped her forms into a pile of other questionnaires, leaving a few pages in between. That way, no one at the agency would notice that Magenta and Daniella had the same address but different last names.

Jessica winked at Elizabeth as they left.

"Just you watch, Liz. This is really going to be something."

Elizabeth rolled her eyes. Jessica was courting disaster, as usual. It was going to be something, all right, Elizabeth thought. Something disastrous.

Two

Jessica parked the red Fiat convertible she shared with Elizabeth at the top of the Wakefields' driveway. She had barely turned the motor off before she leapt out of the car and bounded to the front door.

Elizabeth followed her twin and watched as she reached into the mailbox and removed a jumble of letters, magazines, and flyers. She stood by patiently while Jessica sorted through everything.

"Hey, what's this?" Jessica cried, pulling a business-size envelope out of the stack of mail. She read the address and let out an excited laugh. "Look, Liz. It's from Lovestruck to Daniella Fromage."

"That was fast," Elizabeth said. "It's only Friday, and they already sent you something."

13

Jessica ripped open the envelope and pulled out the letter. "Listen to this! 'Your perfect match is Pierre Du Lac,' it says. 'He was born in France, has traveled extensively on the Continent and in Europe—' "

"The Continent *and* Europe?" Elizabeth broke in, looking puzzled. "Isn't that the same thing?"

Jessica shrugged. "So they goofed. Let me finish it." Her eyes devoured the information in front of her. "It says he speaks four languages, plans to be a novelist or a museum curator, plays the piano, and loves jogging and sailing. His favorite foods are truffles and foie gras. And he's dying to meet me!"

With a gasp of pure ecstasy, Jessica pressed the letter to her chest. "I've got goose bumps," she said. "Tell me the truth, Liz. Doesn't he sound fantastic? He must be so sophisticated!"

"I guess," Elizabeth agreed. Her mouth turned up in a wry smile. "He sounds pretty nice."

"Nice?" Jessica gave her twin a withering look. "I have struck *gold*, Liz. You're just jealous."

Elizabeth laughed and shook her head. "Right, Jess. I'm dying of jealousy. Can we go in now?"

"All right, all right," Jessica muttered. She unlocked the front door and rushed inside.

"I have to call the agency right away to tell

them Pierre can have my phone number," she shouted, racing toward the kitchen to use the phone. Mrs. Wakefield worked full time as an interior designer, so the twins usually had the house to themselves in the afternoons. At the moment, Jessica was glad her mother wasn't around to overhear her phone call about Daniella and Pierre.

An excited bark greeted her as she stepped into the kitchen, and a boisterous golden Labrador retriever hurled himself at her.

"Hi, Prince Albert," Jessica gasped as she pushed his huge paws off her stomach. The family dog was obviously glad to see her. He was so glad, in fact, that every time Jessica tried to move past him to get to the phone, he planted himself in front of her, waiting to be hugged. Half groaning and half giggling, Jessica shoved the big dog away and grabbed the telephone. She read the phone number off the Lovestruck letterhead and dialed.

"Good afternoon, Lovestruck."

"Hello!" Jessica said breathlessly. Prince Albert put his paws up on the counter and panted into the telephone. "This is Daniella Fromage— quit that, Prince Albert!—you sent me a letter about Pierre Du Lac."

"Yes? Is anything wrong?"

15

"No! I want you to go ahead and give him my phone number!" Jessica went on. "Prince, not now!"

There was a pause. Then the receptionist said, "I hope you don't mind my asking, but if you've got a prince after you, why do you need us?"

Jessica covered the mouthpiece with one hand so the woman on the other end wouldn't hear her laughing. Finally she said in a mock serious voice, "I'm bored with him, that's why! All he ever wants to do is chase tennis balls."

Laughing, she hung up the phone. "Get down, Prince Albert," she scolded him fondly. Then she sat down and reread the letter about Pierre.

"I hope I'm sophisticated enough for him," she said to Elizabeth as her twin came into the kitchen.

Elizabeth opened the refrigerator. "Well, you could always take a crash course in culture," she teased.

Jessica grinned. "Hey, that's not a bad idea." She pulled the phone book toward her and looked up Suzanne Hanlon's number. Since Daniella was modeled on Suzanne, it made sense to go right to the original for help.

"Who are you calling?" Elizabeth asked in surprise.

Jessica's eyes sparkled as she dialed. "You'll

16

see." After a few rings, a man's voice answered. Jessica knew it was Mason, the Hanlons' butler. "Hi," she chirped. "This is Jessica Wakefield, from Suzanne's sorority. Is she home?"

"One moment, please, miss."

While Mason went off to find Suzanne, Jessica rehearsed what she would say. They were in the same exclusive sorority, Phi Beta Alpha, but that didn't mean they were good friends—in fact, Jessica thought Suzanne was a snob. But Suzanne knew all the things Daniella was supposed to know, so Jessica needed Suzanne—it was as simple as that.

"Jessica? Hi." Suzanne sounded a bit surprised.

Instantly Jessica put on her sweetest manner. "Hi, Suzanne! I was just trying to decide who the most sophisticated person I know is. You know why?"

"No." Suzanne sounded even more surprised.

"Well, I met this boy," Jessica said in a friendly tone. "And he's *so* cultured. He's been all over the world. I feel kind of dumb next to him, and I've always envied how poised and elegant you are. I was hoping—"

Jessica broke off. She was hoping that piling on the flattery would get to Suzanne's ego and that Suzanne would be the one to suggest the crash course in culture.

"You want a few pointers?" Suzanne asked. She did sound flattered. "Well, I guess I could help you out with some suggestions."

"Oh, would you?" Jessica said. "That's so nice of you! If there's anyone who knows how to act around a really sophisticated guy, it has to be you!"

"I *have* spent my whole life with people like that, of course," Suzanne agreed.

Jessica stuck her tongue out at the phone. Suzanne's condescending attitude was hard to take, but it would be worth it. "I know, that's why I asked you," Jessica gushed.

"Do you want to come over tomorrow?"

"That would be great!" Jessica said.

"OK. Come over around ten. Bye-bye." Suzanne hung up.

" 'Bye-bye,' " Jessica mimicked, hanging up the phone. She gave Elizabeth a thumbs-up sign. "Thanks for a great idea, Liz."

At precisely ten o'clock on Saturday morning, Jessica drove up the Hanlons' winding driveway. Punctuality wasn't usually one of Jessica's strong points, but when she needed something she could manage to be on time. After parking next to a gleaming Rolls Royce, Jessica knocked on the front door.

"Good morning, miss," said the gloomy-looking butler who answered the door. "Miss Hanlon is expecting you in the solarium."

"Thanks," Jessica replied breezily. She tried not to ogle the fine antiques and lavishly decorated rooms as she followed Mason through the house. She knew it wasn't classy to ogle.

Suzanne was sitting in a big white wicker chair in the sunroom. "Hi, Jessica," she said, standing up. "Thanks, Mason."

The butler gave a dignified bow, then left the room. Jessica gave Suzanne a sunny smile. "Is he always so cheerful?"

"No. You got him on a good day," Suzanne shot back, grinning. She smoothed down the pretty blue linen skirt she had on and pointed to another wicker chair. "Have a seat."

"Thanks." Jessica tried to put on her most humble, hopeful expression. "It's so nice of you to help me out, Suzanne," she said. "I knew I could count on you. If anyone can teach me about culture, it's you."

"Forget it," the other girl replied. A faint blush of pleasure colored Suzanne's cheeks as she reached for a stack of leather albums. "Let's start with these."

"Scrapbooks?" Jessica asked, curious.

"Albums," Suzanne corrected her firmly. She

opened the first one. "These are pictures from one of our vacations in Italy. We stayed in this villa here, overlooking the olive groves."

Jessica eagerly drank in all the details in the photographs. She saw the Hanlons relaxing on a balcony, strolling through manicured gardens, and standing in front of spectacular scenery. In spite of herself, she was impressed. These were pictures of a sophisticated, cultured life that she could only dream about.

"Nice," she murmured. "Tell me all about it."

Four hours later, Jessica finished her third glass of iced tea. She studied the painting Suzanne was pointing to in *The Impressionists' Era*, and tried to look as though she remembered who painted it.

"It's, uh, Manet, right?" she said.

Suzanne shook her head. "*Monet*. You can't mistake the style."

"Oh. Right." Jessica nodded and tried to look intrigued.

But the truth was, impressionism seemed to her to be nothing more than a fancy way of describing blurry pictures. How could she be expected to tell one artist from another? Pierre

Du Lac was interested in art, though, so Jessica was determined to be knowledgeable about it.

She rattled the ice in her empty glass. Her head was spinning. The opera they were listening to seemed to have reached a climactic scene. The soprano was coughing and moaning in Italian, while some guy kept singing, "Mimi! Mimi!" At this point Jessica had crammed so many facts into her mind that she thought they must be spilling out of her ears.

"Are you ready to watch the Truffaut film now?" Suzanne asked.

Jessica didn't think she could bear one more minute of letting Suzanne show off how sophisticated she was. With a sad smile, Jessica shook her head. "I don't think I can," she said, her voice filled with regret. "I promised my sister I'd bring the car back by two-thirty." The lie rolled easily off Jessica's tongue. In fact, she wanted to go to the beach, but Suzanne didn't have to know that.

"Oh. OK," Suzanne said. She picked up a Neiman-Marcus shopping bag. "You can borrow these things as long as you need them," she added.

The bag contained several silk blouses, two Chanel purses, two designer scarves, a pair of Gucci shoes, and some other accessories. Jessica had convinced Suzanne they would make her more sophisticated.

"Thanks, Suzanne," Jessica said, standing up and taking the Neiman-Marcus bag. "I really appreciate it."

"No problem," Suzanne told her generously. "Any time."

Still smiling, Jessica followed Suzanne to the front door. Once she was back in the Fiat, Jessica relaxed.

"Look out, Pierre," she murmured, starting up the car. "Prepare to meet your perfect match."

Elizabeth was practicing her recorder when she heard Jessica bounding up the stairs. She paused, waiting for her twin to burst in and tell her the latest news. Jessica always had to share her experiences instantly.

"That girl should take the hangers out of her shirts before she wears them," Jessica announced, strolling in and flopping onto Elizabeth's bed. "She's so stuck up it isn't even funny."

"But that doesn't stop you from picking her brains," Elizabeth pointed out.

Her sister giggled and made a sour face. "What a disgusting thing to say! Anyway—" The phone rang, cutting Jessica off. "I'll get it," she said, reaching for the extension on Elizabeth's nightstand. "Hello?"

Elizabeth watched her sister's expression go from bored to dazzling in one second.

"Yes, this is Daniella!" Jessica exclaimed. She looked at Elizabeth, widening her eyes and nodding. "It's Pierre!" she mouthed.

Then Jessica's smile changed to a dreamy expression, and a faraway look came into her eyes. "Uh-huh—I mean, yes, of course. That sounds lovely. Next Friday? Well, I'm attending a poetry reading after school, but I'll be free by seven."

Elizabeth rolled her eyes. Sometimes Jessica was just too much!

"Chez Sam? In Pacific Shores? Yes, it's charming," Jessica murmured. Her voice was throatier, and Elizabeth thought she could hear the trace of an accent. It was obviously another facet of Daniella.

When Jessica hung up the phone, she sat very still for a moment. Then she threw herself backward on the bed and kicked her feet up in the air. *"Yee-ow!"* she crowed. "He sounds so—so *perfect!*"

Elizabeth just shook her head.

Three

Jessica let her arms and legs hang over both sides of the bed. She let out a blissful sigh. "My life is now about to begin," she announced.

"Congratulations," her sister replied wryly. "I hope Daniella and Pierre will be very happy together."

Something in Elizabeth's voice caught Jessica's attention. She lifted her head to look at her twin. "What is it?" she said. "I know there's something you're not telling me."

Elizabeth arched her eyebrows. "When I went out to get the mail today, I found something for Magenta Galaxy. It's in your—"

Jessica didn't wait for Elizabeth to finish. She sprang off the bed and raced through the bathroom that connected their rooms. Propped up on her bureau was another business-size envelope from Lovestruck.

Breathless, she tore it open and read through the letter. Her heart was pounding wildly. "Liz! You've got to hear this!" she announced.

Elizabeth appeared in the bathroom doorway. "OK, Magenta. Shoot."

"It's a boy named Brett S." Jessica began ecstatically.

"Just S?" Elizabeth asked. "That's a pretty weird last name. But so is Galaxy, so I guess you're a perfect match."

Jessica stuck her tongue out at Elizabeth. "Sarcasm will get you nowhere. Just listen: He wants to be a race car driver or a rock guitarist, or both. He believes in living life to the max. He says he's tall, dark, and wild, and likes his girls to be tall, blond, and wild. That's me!" Jessica gasped, her eyes sparkling.

"You mean, that's Magenta," Elizabeth corrected her.

"Right, right. Magenta." Jessica skimmed the letter again. "Oh, Liz. He sounds so exciting! I knew it was a good idea to use two different personalities."

Jessica ignored Elizabeth's skeptical look. Once Jessica had two exciting, captivating new boyfriends, she was sure her twin would have to agree that the plan had been brilliant.

"I'm calling the agency right now," she decided. "It's not too late for them to call Brett and tell him he can call me. I mean Magenta."

"Jess, why don't you just be yourself?" Elizabeth asked. "I know this isn't going to work."

Jessica put her hands on her twin's shoulders. "Liz, I realize you're trying to be my big sister and take care of me, but it's going to be perfect. I promise."

"You're sure about that, huh?" Elizabeth said, shaking her head.

Jessica grinned. "Positive. And now if you'll excuse me, I have to make a very important telephone call."

Jessica woke up early on Sunday morning. She sat up in bed, pulled her knees up to her chin, and stared at the telephone on the floor.

"Ring, ring, ring," she chanted.

Since she had called Lovestruck to say Brett S. could call Magenta Galaxy for a date, Jessica was sure the phone would ring at any minute. She wanted to be the one to answer it so her parents wouldn't say, "Magenta *who*?"

Jessica already had a mental picture of Brett.

He would be tall and lanky, with a leather jacket and swept-back black hair, a pair of piercing dark eyes, and a very kissable mouth. She got goose bumps just thinking about him.

Of course, when she talked to him she would have to be very cool, very aloof. Magenta Galaxy was not the type of girl to gush on the telephone or talk about being a cheerleader and going to school dances. Magenta had to be—like Dana Larson.

Jessica frowned in concentration. She had never been friends with Dana Larson. It wasn't that she didn't like the pretty blond. Jessica admired her. She had her own style of dressing, and Jessica envied the way Dana could stand up in front of a crowd as the lead singer of The Droids, Sweet Valley High's premier rock band. It was just that they didn't have very much in common.

But that was all going to change. Assuming Brett called—and Jessica was confident he would—Jessica would have to spend some time with Dana.

Hanging around the house all day waiting for the phone to ring was frustrating. Instead of going to the beach with Lila Fowler and Cara Walker, two of her best friends, Jessica lounged by the pool in the backyard, the cordless phone by her right hand. Finally, around four o'clock, the phone rang.

"Hello?" Jessica said. She was careful to keep the excitement out of her voice.

"Hi, is Magenta there?"

A shiver of delight ran up Jessica's spine. She settled back comfortably in her lounge chair. "This is Magenta," she replied. "Who's this?"

"Brett S. I think we should meet."

Jessica's eyes widened. "You don't waste time, do you?" she marveled. "I like that."

"I know what I want," Brett said. His voice sounded just the way Jessica had imagined it— cool, sulky, and sexy. "How about next Saturday? We could go to the Rock Spot."

"The Rock Spot? Let me think about that for a second." Jessica paused. She wanted to play it cool and keep Brett waiting for a few moments. If she was going to *be* Magenta, she had to start acting like her.

Finally she said, "That sounds great. What time will you pick me up?" she asked.

"How does eight o'clock sound?" Brett asked.

"Terrific." Jessica laughed. She gave Brett her address, then she hung up.

Touché, Magenta, she told herself smugly. She stretched her legs and grinned. Magenta definitely knew how to play it cool.

Now Jessica had less than one week to find out how Magenta did everything else.

"This is the Blue Frogs, right?" Jessica asked Dana Larson. She tried to concentrate on the jangling guitar chords coming out of Dana's portable tape deck. They were sitting at a table in one corner of the Sweet Valley High cafeteria, eating lunch and starting Jessica's initiation into superhip culture.

Dana ran a hand through her cropped blond hair. "Blues Hogs," she said patiently. She gave Jessica a skeptical look. "Why are you so interested in this stuff all of a sudden, anyway?"

"I told you," Jessica replied, smiling. "True love. You believe in that, right? Say, could I borrow those bracelets?"

Dana looked down at her wrists. She was wearing four thick black bangles on each arm. They went perfectly with her skintight black pants, black and white-checked shoes, and lime green T-shirt. In one ear she wore a guitar pick dangling from a silver wire. She looked up again and grinned. "Sure. In the name of true love."

"Great." Jessica held out her hands while Dana pulled the bracelets off. "The other thing

I wanted to know about is all those music clubs you go to. What are they like?"

Dana took a swallow of her soda. "Which ones? Around here or in L.A.?"

Jessica did some quick thinking. "L.A.," she decided.

"OK. First there's Jumping Jimmy's," Dana began. "They showcase new talent every Thursday night . . ."

Elizabeth put her pen down, squeezed her eyes shut, and covered her ears. "Jessica!" she muttered. The music was so loud Elizabeth could feel it vibrating in her bones.

With a groan of frustration, Elizabeth stood up from her desk and went through the bathroom. In the doorway of Jessica's room, she stopped in shock.

Under normal circumstances, Jessica's room looked like a hurricane had swept through it. At the moment it was even worse than usual. Piled on the bed were expensive, designer accessories mixed in with weird, neon-colored costume jewelry. There were maps of Europe and posters of French paintings taped on the walls, and cassettes tossed across the floor. Jessica was lying on her back in the middle of it, nod-

31

ding her head in time with the Psychedelic Over-
tones and studying her French book.

Elizabeth shook her head in bewilderment.
Between Dana's punk rock and Suzanne's high-
brow culture, it looked as though Jessica were
becoming truly schizophrenic at last.

Finally Jessica noticed her. Over the music
she shouted, "Hi, Liz!" Then she went back to
mouthing French phrases under her breath and
tapping her foot.

"Jess, can you turn the music down?" Elizabeth begged. "I can't hear myself think!"

Jessica lowered her book. "What?"

"I said, turn it *down!*"

Jessica leaned over and switched off her tape
deck. "What?"

"Never mind." Elizabeth sighed. She picked
up an expensive cream-colored silk blouse in
one hand and nudged at a pair of black motorcycle boots with her toe. "Do these go together?"

"Of course not," Jessica scoffed. "The blouse
is Suzanne's, and I'm wearing that on Friday
night with Pierre. The boots are Dana's, and I'll
wear those on Saturday when I go out with
Brett."

"Right." Elizabeth leaned against the doorway, running her hand over the silky smooth-
ness of the blouse. After a moment, she said,

"Listen, Jess, don't you think it's kind of useless, all this studying you're doing? You're trying to turn yourself into something you're not."

"I'm not yet, but I could be," her twin insisted in a confident voice. "Why shouldn't I go for something I want? You never get anything if you don't take a chance."

Elizabeth bit her lower lip. "I know. That's not what I meant. It's just that—" She broke off, weighing her words carefully.

"Just what?" Jessica pushed. "Do you think I'll blow it?"

"No." Elizabeth felt her cheeks redden. "I wasn't trying to insult you," she apologized. "I just don't want you to end up getting hurt."

Jessica made a face. "You always say that, Liz. You never take risks. You just play it safe so you don't 'end up getting hurt.' "

"So? What's wrong with that?" Elizabeth asked. She felt embarrassed and guilty. When Jessica put it that way, it made her seem dull and spiritless. "What's wrong with knowing your limitations?"

Jessica stood up and went to her bureau. She found a hairbrush and began vigorously brushing her glossy blond hair. "That's so typical of you, Liz. It's just like that dress you wanted so much for the dance. You *know* it's perfect for you, but because it doesn't fit your budget you just make yourself forget about it."

Elizabeth met her twin's eyes in the mirror. She didn't know what to say.

"So you won't get it," Jessica went on. "But now you'll be disappointed with whatever you do wear to the dance because you'll always wish you had gotten that dress."

There was an awkward silence. Elizabeth was deep in thought. *Am I really a coward?* she wondered. When she took a hard, critical look at herself, she began to think she was. She had one steady boyfriend, conservative tastes, modest ambitions—in fact, she was as predictable as Jessica was adventurous. And she wasn't sure being steady as a rock was all that great.

"I'm not afraid to take risks," Jessica continued after a moment. "Maybe it *won't* work out, but at least I'll know for sure. I won't always have to wonder what it would be like to date a boy like Pierre or a boy like Brett. *I'm* going for it."

With that, Jessica turned the tape deck on again and picked up her French book. Elizabeth stood there, torn between following her own good advice and admitting that Jessica had a point. Why shouldn't Jessica learn new things so that she could attract different types of boys?

And why shouldn't she herself borrow the money to buy the dress?

"I guess it could work," Elizabeth said hesitantly.

Jessica didn't hear her. She was busy keeping time with the music and looking up words.

Elizabeth turned and went back to her own room. She propped her chin up on her hands as she sat down at the table she used as a desk. A whirl of thoughts spun through her head.

I'm turning into a real bore, she thought glumly. *I should learn how to be more spontaneous.*

With a firm nod, Elizabeth took out her journal, turned to the first blank page, and wrote in capital letters: DARE TO BE DIFFERENT. Then she snapped her journal shut. From now on, Elizabeth Wakefield was *not* going to look before she leaped.

Four

Jessica drove to Fowler Crest after dinner on Thursday. Lila had promised to help her get ready for her dates with Pierre and Brett. Jessica grinned, remembering what she had told her mother: "I'm going to Lila's to study," she had said. That was the truth. She just hadn't mentioned what it was she was going to study!

Lila was home alone with the housekeeper, Eva. Her parents had divorced when she was little, and her father was frequently away on business, so Lila spent most of her time by herself.

"Let's go up to my room," Lila said in a bored tone of voice. She dragged her feet going up the wide, carpeted staircase.

"What's wrong?" Jessica asked. She regarded

her friend critically. She thought Lila seemed very preoccupied.

Lila shrugged. "Nothing." She let out a dramatic sigh. "It's just that I don't see why you had to go to Suzanne to learn about being sophisticated." Lila sounded hurt.

"Oh." Jessica was momentarily stumped. She knew she had to think of something fast, because Lila could carry a grudge for weeks.

The Fowlers certainly had as much money as the Hanlons did. In fact, George Fowler probably had more money from his computer business than anyone else in Sweet Valley. And it wasn't as though Lila didn't have class, either. It was just that a fortune recently made in silicon chips wasn't the same as generations of wealth and breeding. Suzanne was *old* money, and Jessica was sure that distinction made a difference to someone like Pierre Du Lac.

"It's not that," Jessica explained in her most diplomatic voice. "You know what a culture snob Suzanne is, right? I mean, you're *nothing* like that, Lila. You're so much more real— and—honest."

Lila shrugged again and opened the door to her gigantic bedroom. "I guess," she muttered, but she looked happier.

Breathing a sigh of relief, Jessica tossed her bag onto a pink upholstered chair and flopped onto the canopied bed. "And don't worry. It's not like Suzanne's my good friend or anything. She's really impossible. Now come on, are you going to help me or not?"

"Sure. What do you want me to do?" Lila crossed her legs under her on her bed and toyed with the gold bracelets on her wrist. She looked at Jessica expectantly.

Jessica jumped up, took several folded sheets out of her bag, and handed them to her friend. "Quiz me, OK? Just read one of the names from this list and tell me if I describe it right." She sat down opposite Lila. "Go ahead."

Lila shuffled the pages. "OK. What is an *aubergine*?"

"Eggplant," Jessica answered. She grinned. "Simple. Ask me another."

Lila arched her eyebrows. "Sophisticated people eat eggplant? Is that what you're telling me?"

"They eat *aubergines*," Jessica said with a smirk. "Go on."

"Who is the conductor of the Academy of St. Martin in the Fields?" Lila read, looking skeptical. "What is that? Some kind of prep school?"

Jessica rolled her eyes. "For your information, it just happens to be a very *famous* chamber orchestra, and the conductor is Sir Neville Marriner."

"Exc-u-u-se me," Lila retorted. "Who painted *Starry Night*?"

"That one's simple," Jessica said airily. "Renoir."

"Wrong!" Lila glanced up from the sheet and gave Jessica a challenging look. "It was not Renoir, it was—"

"Don't tell me!" Jessica squeezed her eyes shut in concentration. "Umm . . . Van Gogh!" she cried.

Lila made a sour face. "Right. Say, what do you think of David Hockney?"

"David who?" Jessica sat up, confused. She grabbed the sheets out of Lila's hand and leafed through them anxiously. "That's not on my list."

Her friend shrugged. "So? I'm just asking your opinion."

"I don't want you to ask my opinion," Jessica growled. She slapped the lists down in front of Lila. "Just ask me what's on here."

Shuffling the pages again, Lila said, "All right. But if Pierre asks you if you like Hockney, you can't say he's not on your list!"

Jessica folded her arms across her chest. Lila had a point. But there was no way she could learn *everything* in such a short time. She would just have to be careful to keep the conversation on subjects she had studied.

"Do you think this guy is really worth it?" Lila asked, leaning back on one elbow. "I mean, he's just another boy."

Jessica shook her head. "He is not just another boy, Lila. You read the letter yourself. He's my ideal partner."

"Yeah, right," Lila scoffed.

Jessica ignored her friend. To her it sounded as if Lila was just envious. With a patient smile, she said, "Just read the list, please."

"Fine," Lila said. She skimmed the pages. "I'll ask you some stuff for Brett, too. Who was Abbie Hoffman?"

Jessica grimaced. "Give me a hint."

Lila shook her head silently.

"Oh, come on! No, wait, wait. Just let me think. I have to concentrate," Jessica said, closing her eyes for a moment. "Isn't he lead guitarist for the Grateful Dead?" she ventured.

"Not quite," Lila said in a lazy voice. "Try again."

Jessica searched her mind frantically for several moments. Her head was so crowded with names and facts that she couldn't even remember if Flaubert was an author or a kind of cheese or whether Maximum Outrage was a rock group or a perfume. Frustrated, Jessica said, "Forget that one. Ask me another."

"For your information," Lila said, "Abbie Hoffman was that sixties radical hippie who died in 1989. Even *I* know that."

Jessica looked at the ceiling. "OK, OK. Abbie Hoffman, dead hippie. Ask me another."

"What's the best place to buy vintage records in Sweet Valley?"

"Tune Town, on Fifth Street," Jessica answered immediately. "Ha! Got that one. Come on, let's do the whole thing."

Lila tipped her head to one side. "Boy, I sure hope these guys are worth it," she said.

"They will be," Jessica said, smiling confidently. "Both of them. And tomorrow night is my first test!"

At five-thirty on Friday, Elizabeth started getting ready to go out. She and Todd were meeting some of their friends at the Dairi Burger. After dinner they would all go to a movie together. As Jessica would say, it was "typical high school." Elizabeth was still determined to be more spontaneous, but even so she was really looking forward to the evening. At least she could order ginger ale instead of her usual root beer, she told herself with a self-mocking smile.

"Liz! Help!" The desperate shriek came from Jessica's bedroom.

Elizabeth finished putting in her earrings. Desperate shrieks from Jessica were commonplace. "What? What's wrong?" she called out.

"You've got to help me!" Jessica wailed. "This is a crisis!"

Shaking her head, Elizabeth went through the bathroom, stepped over a pile of damp towels, and found Jessica standing by the bed, clutching a towel around her. Scattered everywhere were Suzanne Hanlon's expensive blouses, scarves, and accessories.

"What's wrong?" Elizabeth asked.

"I need help," Jessica said. "I'm so nervous I don't know what to wear!"

Elizabeth surveyed the scene. The makings of at least a dozen glamorous outfits were draped everywhere. As long as everything wasn't hopelessly wrinkled, she thought that Jessica should be able to pull together something beautiful and stylish.

"How about this blouse?" Elizabeth suggested, picking up the cream-colored silk one she had noticed before. "You have those navy blue linen pants. They would look great with this."

Jessica's eyes opened wide. "Pants? Don't you think that's too casual?"

"Well, it's Friday night, after all," Elizabeth pointed out. "You don't want to look too dressy."

Jessica snapped her fingers. "You're right," she agreed. "I don't want to look like I'm wearing my best clothes. I have to look casual but sophisticated, as if this is just another dinner at a fantastic restaurant, no big deal."

Elizabeth tried not to look too exasperated. After all, Jessica was really serious about dating Pierre. Just because she was acting a little crazy was no reason for Elizabeth to be discouraging. If Jessica wanted to change her whole image, that was her business. It was certainly adventurous, and Elizabeth had to admit that that could be a good thing.

While Jessica stepped into her tailored blue pants, Elizabeth searched through the clothing on her twin's bed. A square silk scarf in red, blue, and gold caught her eye. She made a triangle out of it and held it against the blouse. It looked terrific.

"Oh, that's great!" Jessica exclaimed when she saw the effect. "And it'll be perfect with that little red bag of Suzanne's and my blue suede flats."

In a few minutes Jessica was fully dressed and preening in front of her mirror. "How do I look?" she asked, her voice anxious.

Elizabeth smiled. "You look very elegant," she said sincerely. She gave her sister a hug.

"Really?" Jessica looked at herself again and turned from side to side. "Do you really think so?"

"Yes!" Elizabeth laughed. "Really."

Jessica grinned excitedly. Her eyes looked brilliant. "Thanks, Liz. This outfit is perfect! You're wonderful!"

"Forget it," Elizabeth said.

Shaking her head, Jessica replied, "No, I really mean it. You're the best sister in the whole world. And you know what?" Jessica exclaimed cheerfully. "I'm going to do you a *huge* favor."

"Oh, yeah?" Elizabeth eyed her twin with suspicion. "Am I going to like this *huge* favor?"

"You're going to love it," Jessica answered smugly. "I've been thinking about it, and I've decided to split the cost of that dress with you. I insist," she added when Elizabeth started to protest. "You know it's the perfect dress for you, and I think you should have it in time for the Valentine's Day dance. Besides, since it looks so good on you, I'll be able to wear it, too."

Elizabeth didn't know what to say. Jessica could be a real pain sometimes, but then she would turn around and do something so sweet! Jessica was absolutely unpredictable, and that was what made her so much fun. Elizabeth went over to her sister and gave her another big hug.

"You should listen to your little sister," Jessica teased. "Sometimes you just have to go for it. When opportunity knocks and all that."

"Right," Elizabeth said. "Thanks, Jess. I owe you a big one."

"I know," Jessica replied, grinning mischievously. "I'll think of a way for you to pay me back, don't worry."

"I know you will." Elizabeth laughed. "And I'll do it, whatever it is. Now let's figure out what Daniella would do with her hair. You have to leave for Chez Sam any minute. Monsieur Du Lac is waiting for you!"

"Yikes!" Jessica let out a screech and raced to the bathroom.

Laughing, Elizabeth followed. Crazy and tempestuous as Jessica was, Elizabeth loved her. And as for returning a favor, that would be easy enough—she hoped.

Five

"Don't mess up, don't mess up," Jessica chanted quietly to herself as she drove to Chez Sam. She was terrified that she would say something stupid and naive, something that would let Pierre know she was faking it.

As she pulled into the parking lot and saw the awning with Chez Sam in flowing script, she felt her stomach flip-flop.

Then she parked the car, jumped out, smoothed the creases out of her linen pants, and walked slowly, elegantly, and above all *sophisticatedly* to the entrance of the restaurant. Inside, she checked her reflection in the full-length mirror. Her hair was pulled back neatly and clipped with a wide gold barrette, the scarf was artfully

49

tied over the silk blouse, and the suede shoes looked exactly right with the outfit.

Perfect, Jessica decided with a satisfied smile.

"Good evening, Mademoiselle," the maitre d' greeted her. He bowed. "Can I help you?"

Jessica drew a deep breath. Her hands were shaking slightly. "Yes. I'm meeting Mr. Du Lac. Is he here yet?"

"But of course. Please follow me." The maître d' turned and moved smoothly through the crowded dining room.

Following behind, Jessica tried to look poised and elegant, but she couldn't tell if it was working. She felt a little shaky.

Because the waiter was just in front of her, she didn't see Pierre until she had gotten all the way to the table. As he stood up to greet her, Jessica felt her heart flutter.

"Hello, Daniella? I'm Pierre," he said.

The boy standing in front of her was everything Jessica dreamed he would be. He was tall and slim, with a narrow, sensitive face and light brown hair. Dark eyelashes framed a pair of bright blue eyes. His navy blazer and gray pants looked impeccable, and his white shirt complemented his tan perfectly. He looked as though he had just stepped out of the pages of a fashion magazine.

"I'm pleased to meet you," Jessica murmured, slipping into her seat. She took a moment to collect her wits before looking up. When she did, she gave Pierre her most sparkling smile.

"So, here we are," she said. Then she immediately berated herself for saying something so trite.

"Here we are," Pierre repeated. He smiled, and an adorable dimple appeared in his cheek.

Captivated, Jessica searched for something witty to say as she unfolded her napkin. Her mind was a blank. All her careful studying had gone right out of her head. "Have you been here before?" she asked finally.

"Well, no," Pierre replied. He smiled again, his blue eyes crinkling at the corners. "This is my first time."

"Oh, you probably go to Le Chou Farci all the time," Jessica said quickly. That was the most expensive restaurant in the area. According to Suzanne, the Hanlons ate there once a week. "So do I, but it's nice to try something new, isn't it?"

Pierre was still smiling. He nodded. "Yes. It sure is. I guess we're both trying something new tonight," he added.

"Oh. Of course." Jessica decided he had just made a subtle joke about their date, and she let out a peal of laughter. *"Vive la différence,"* she said. She was pretty sure that was a pertinent French phrase.

Pierre just smiled and picked up his menu. His hands were long and artistic-looking. "What would you like to eat?" he asked. He frowned as he scanned the offerings.

Flustered, Jessica opened her menu, too. Pierre was obviously the quiet type: he seemed to say more with smiles than with words. She decided she would have to be even more careful to impress him. And since he was so drop-dead gorgeous, she was absolutely determined to impress him.

The menu was all in French. Jessica was terrified for a moment when she didn't recognize any of the words. Then she remembered that *thon* was tuna fish. She didn't want to make the mistake of ordering something that turned out to be calves' brains. She knew the French ate some pretty horrible things, but she wasn't willing to be *that* sophisticated.

"I'll have the *thon aux herbes,"* she said, pronouncing the words carefully. "I love tuna."

"That sounds great," Pierre agreed. He nodded and closed his menu. "I'll have the same." Just then their waiter glided up to the table. "We'll both have the tuna," he announced.

"Very good, monsieur," the waiter murmured. He slipped away again.

Jessica was slightly surprised that Pierre had ordered in English instead of in French. Then, as though reading her mind, Pierre explained, "He's French Canadian. I spoke with him before you got here, and our accents are so different! It just seemed simpler to speak to him in English."

"Of course," Jessica said, smiling pleasantly. She was really impressed. She couldn't wait to tell Lila all about how sophisticated and cultured Pierre was!

"So, tell me about you," Pierre invited. "What does Daniella want from life?"

Jessica toyed with her fork nervously and then put it down. It didn't seem very poised to play with the silverware. "Well, there's so much," she said. "Sometimes I feel life isn't long enough to do everything I want to do—read all the poetry, hear all the symphonies, *drown* myself in the dance."

"Which dance?" Pierre asked, a puzzled expression on his face.

For a moment, Jessica was paralyzed. Wasn't it correct to say *the dance* instead of saying *ballet* or *dancing*? But then she realized that Pierre might not be familiar with that term, having spent so much time living in Europe. There must be some other phrase for it in French.

"All dance," she said with an aloof smile. "Balanchine, Baryshnikov—"

"Yes, I know what you mean," Pierre agreed, returning Jessica's smile. "It's wonderful."

Jessica breathed an inward sigh of relief. She had thought she might have blown it, but the crisis was past. Relaxing a bit, she said, "And cinema, too. Don't you love Fellini?"

"Definitely. Especially with white clam sauce and Parmesan cheese," Pierre replied after a brief hesitation. "And garlic bread."

It took Jessica a few heartbeats to realize he was making another subtle, esoteric joke—pretending that Fellini was a kind of pasta! She let out a tinkle of laughter and sipped her water.

"Have you read Verdet's poetry?" Pierre asked. A serious expression crossed his aristocratic face. "I really think it's the most important work being done today. Besides Rolfenhausen, of course."

Jessica searched her memory frantically. Had Suzanne told her anything about Verdet or Rolfenhausen? She didn't think she had ever heard of them at all. At first she didn't know what to say. Then she decided that sometimes admitting ignorance was just as effective as being knowledgeable.

"I'm afraid I don't know Rolfenhausen," she said with a winning smile. "Where does his— her?—work appear?"

"Baroness Rolfenhausen," Pierre explained. "Mostly in the European literary journals. American audiences don't know her well at all."

"Oh, I know what you mean," Jessica gushed. "Most Americans are so ignorant about poetry they wouldn't know Millay from Dickinson," she went on, mentioning the only two names she was really sure were poets.

Pierre blinked. "Right. Oh, here's our dinner."

Jessica imagined there was a trace of relief in his voice, and she wondered if he realized she was faking it. But he certainly seemed to like her, judging from all the smiling he did.

Just relax, she told herself firmly. *Don't get carried away.*

"*Bon appetit*," she said.

"Excuse me?" Pierre said, wrinkling his forehead.

Jessica blushed. "I know my accent isn't very good," she mumbled. "I probably shouldn't even try to speak French because I'll just embarrass myself."

"Oh, no. I'm sorry, I just didn't hear you,"

Pierre said. He gave her a winning smile and raised his water glass. "Here's to Daniella."

Jessica felt a flush of pleasure. She raised her glass and clinked it with his. Keeping up appearances was hard work, but as far as Jessica was concerned, Pierre Du Lac was definitely worth it. And when their dinner was over and Pierre asked her to go out again, Jessica realized her studying had really paid off!

"I'd love to," she told him as they strolled out to the parking lot. "What did you have in mind?"

"I thought maybe a film at the Odeon," Pierre suggested, naming Sweet Valley's revival movie theater. "There are several important films playing now."

Jessica took a deep breath. She knew it meant spending another evening struggling to appear cultured and sophisticated. And if he really knew a lot about foreign films, she would have to work exceptionally hard. But if they were at a movie, they wouldn't have to talk that much. And of course, movie theaters were always romantic!

"That would be wonderful," Jessica replied.

She wondered briefly about the doubtful note she thought she sensed in his voice. Was he still not sure whether she was really as sophisticated as she was trying to seem? She decided to get in a few more good references before the night was over.

"I'm busy on Monday and Tuesday," she said, thinking fast. "There's a chamber music concert on Monday, and then on Tuesday I'm going to an art history lecture at the community college."

Pierre looked impressed. "Well, how about Wednesday then?" he asked.

"Fine," Jessica said, congratulating herself. They stopped by the red Fiat. "This is my car," she said.

He looked at her in the dim light. Jessica wondered if he would kiss her hand, or kiss her on both cheeks the way the French did in movies. Her pulse raced as she looked up into his dreamy blue eyes. Nobody had ever kissed her hand before. She hoped he would kiss her hand *and* both cheeks. It would be so European.

"Good night, Daniella," he said huskily.

Jessica swallowed and tipped her head back. "Good night."

"I'll call you about Wednesday," Pierre said.

"OK." Jessica waited.

Then Pierre quickly kissed her lips, turned, and walked away.

Jessica stood rooted to the spot. Slowly she

brought one hand up to touch her mouth, and she felt herself start to smile. Sighing, she climbed into the Fiat. She couldn't wait to tell Elizabeth how perfectly it had worked out.

Of course, thinking about Wednesday night gave her a few misgivings. But there was plenty of time to read movie reviews and ask Suzanne more questions before then. Jessica was sure she had nothing to worry about.

Elizabeth heard her sister walk down the hall past her bedroom. "Hi, Jess!" she called out. "How did your date with Pierre go?"

"Hey, I didn't know you were home already." Jessica poked her head in the doorway.

Elizabeth was painting her toenails bright red. "The movie was terrible, and I decided it was stupid to sit there and watch it anyway, so we left early," she explained. "And Todd and I were both tired, so he went home a little while ago. So, tell me all about Pierre."

"Well. . . ." Jessica came in and sank down on the edge of Elizabeth's bed. Her eyes were starry. "He is simply the most romantic, sophisticated guy I've ever met," she said, sighing blissfully. "Handsome, intelligent, cultured, fascinating—"

"Details, details," Elizabeth prompted. She nudged Jessica with a toe she hadn't painted yet.

Jessica shrugged. "What can I say, Liz? It was wonderful. I can honestly say that signing up at Lovestruck was the smartest thing I ever did."

"So you're not giving me any details, huh?" Elizabeth sat back against her pillows and grinned. "I'll just take your word for it."

Her sister smiled dreamily. "That's right. Just imagine the most wonderful night of your life and multiply that by a hundred. That's what it was like."

"You didn't say anything dumb, like London is the capital of West Germany?" Elizabeth teased. "No terrible *faux pas*? You didn't use the wrong fork?"

"Are you kidding?" Jessica gave Elizabeth a scornful look. "I was perfect."

"I'm sure," Elizabeth said. She still thought it was silly for Jessica to go through such a charade. But obviously her twin was well satisfied with the results.

"Hey," Jessica said after a moment. She was staring at Elizabeth's feet with a baffled expression. "What are you doing?"

Elizabeth smiled sheepishly. "Don't you like it?"

"Well, I guess," her sister replied. She raised her eyebrows. "You just never did that before, that's all."

"I'm doing something different," Elizabeth explained. She shrugged and regarded her crimson toenails thoughtfully. It wasn't exactly a major adventure to paint her toenails, but it was a start. "I like it."

Jessica pushed herself up off the bed and began untying her scarf. "Well, I'm going to bed. You uncultured types can only dream of the kind of happiness I found tonight. Good night," she said in a faraway voice, and she drifted away.

Elizabeth giggled. Jessica loved being mysterious. But when the time came, Elizabeth knew she would find out all about Pierre Du Lac. Jessica could never keep anything to herself for very long.

Six

On Saturday afternoon Elizabeth and Jessica were both out by the pool in the backyard. Jessica was getting in some last-minute tanning, and Elizabeth was reading one of Jessica's fashion magazines. Prince Albert lay nearby in the shade, panting. Hearing the sliding door from the dining room open, Elizabeth glanced over her shoulder.

"Liz?" Alice Wakefield called.

Elizabeth closed the magazine on her finger. "Yes, Mom?"

"Have you seen those dog food coupons anywhere? I'm about to go to the grocery store." Mrs. Wakefield stood in the doorway, shading her eyes against the sun with one hand.

"By the telephone," Elizabeth answered.

"Thanks. Say, Jess," Mrs. Wakefield added. "I just put some clean laundry in your room. Where did all those weird things come from?"

Jessica hoisted herself up on her elbows. "What weird things?"

"Well, that paratrooper outfit, for instance. I never saw that before. And that necklace on your bed, the one made of black rubber and clear plastic—isn't it a little, well, strange?"

Elizabeth and Jessica exchanged a look, and Elizabeth ducked her head to hide her smile. Obviously Jessica had been sorting through the Magenta collection.

"It's just some stuff I borrowed from a friend, Mom," Jessica replied. "That's all."

When their mother went back inside, Elizabeth gave Jessica a wry grin. "It *is* pretty weird-looking, you have to admit," she said.

Jessica shrugged. "So what? What's wrong with looking a little weird sometimes? Besides, those are exactly the kinds of things Magenta would wear. But—?"

"Yes?" Elizabeth asked. She could tell her sister wanted something from her.

Jessica tipped her head to one side. "Can you help me get dressed later? I'm still not sure what to wear. And you did such a good job last night," she added. "I really need your help."

"Gee, thanks. I guess I can always be a fashion consultant if I don't get into college," Elizabeth quipped. But the hopeful expression on her twin's face went straight to her heart. "Sure, I'll help. Just yell when you need me."

"Great," Jessica said, smiling. "Another fabulous night starts in just a few hours."

Elizabeth laughed. "The countdown begins!"

Jessica looked into the bathroom mirror at her glossy blond hair. "I'm serious, Liz. I want a blue streak."

Elizabeth laughed and started shaking the spray can of temporary hair color. "OK. You asked for it."

"I just hope it really washes out," Jessica prayed. She squeezed her eyes shut. "You decide where to put it."

She felt her sister gently tugging on a clump of hair and then heard the *pssst* of the can.

"Yuck, I got some on my hand," Elizabeth said. "All right, Jess. You can look now."

Jessica opened her eyes. Part of her bangs and an inch-wide section of hair on the right side of her head were now a shocking royal blue. Jessica gulped.

"It looks nice with my eyes," she said after a short silence.

Elizabeth didn't say anything.

"Do you think I should have a pink streak, too?" Jessica asked.

"No! Don't overdo it," Elizabeth advised. She started washing the blue color off her hand.

"Well, I should at least use some serious gel," Jessica went on, scowling at her reflection. "I can't just have my hair lie there like it always does."

She yanked open a drawer and started riffling through the contents. At last she found a tube of styling gel and squeezed a huge dollop onto her palm.

"Watch this," she told her sister. With expert touches, she sculpted her hair into a slicked-back wave and brought the blue streak up and around into a coil.

Elizabeth stared in fascination while Jessica's hair was transformed. Then she started laughing. "Here, let me try," she said. She picked up a comb and moved Jessica's part to the extreme right. Then she pulled the blue streak straight back.

Jessica laughed, too. "Yeah, that's better. Now, what accessories should I wear?"

For her outfit, she had chosen tight black bicycle pants, a black tank top, and a red leather jacket she had borrowed from Lila. Almost anything from Dana's collection would look right with the ensemble.

"The guitar pick earring, definitely," Elizabeth said. "And those black bangles."

Jessica grinned at her sister. "You're really getting into this, aren't you?"

"It's like Halloween," Elizabeth replied with a laugh.

"But this is serious, Liz," Jessica insisted, sobering up instantly. "I want to make just the right impression on Brett."

Elizabeth let out a sigh and shook her head.

With another critical look in the mirror, Jessica picked up a black eyeliner pencil and began outlining her eyes with thick, heavy strokes. If she did as good a job being Magenta as she had being Daniella, she was in for another exciting night.

At eight o'clock Jessica was in the living room, peeking out at the street from behind the curtain. Luckily, her parents were out for the evening. She didn't know exactly how wild Brett would look when he arrived, and she didn't want her parents asking any questions. So she was glad they weren't around to see him—or her, for that matter.

Jessica's bangles clicked as she moved the curtain aside, and she began tapping her foot impatiently. She couldn't wait to meet Brett and see if he was as exciting in his way as Pierre was in his. Humming under her breath, she scanned the street in both directions. An old brown Oldsmobile turned the corner and started cruising toward the house. Jessica looked in the other direction, wondering when Brett would show up.

To her surprise, the Oldsmobile sedan pulled up in front of the house.

"Huh?" Jessica said, puzzled.

A tall boy in a black leather jacket got out and started walking toward the front door. Jessica felt her heart jump wildly. It was Brett!

But an Oldsmobile wasn't exactly what she had been expecting. There was something so—so tame about it, so ordinary. Then in a flash she realized it must be some kind of statement. It was so square, it was cool!

Her heart beating with excitement, Jessica raced to the door. Then she slowed down, wiped the eager expression from her face, and casually opened the door.

"Hello," she said.

Brett shook his dark brown hair out of his eyes. "I'm Brett," he announced, eyeing her appreciatively. "I guess you must be Magenta."

"I guess so," Jessica replied with a half smile.

On the outside, she was the picture of cool nonchalance. Inside, she had to restrain herself from jumping up and down and letting out a squeal of enthusiasm. Brett was just the way she expected him to be—tall and lean, with a worn leather jacket that showed off his broad shoulders. Besides the leather jacket he wore a white T-shirt, skintight black jeans, and black motorcycle boots. In spite of the fact that the sun had gone down, he had on a pair of dark sunglasses. When he pushed them up on top of his head, Jessica saw that he had extraordinary gold-brown eyes. She also noticed his strong jaw and high cheekbones. He was definitely the sexiest hard rocker she had ever seen.

"Let's go," she said, stepping outside and pulling the door shut behind her.

With long, athletic strides, Brett headed toward the brown Olds. "This is my old man's car," he started to explain.

"Hey, I think it's a riot," Jessica broke in quickly. She wanted him to see she could look at it the right way. "It makes a real statement— really Mom 'n' Pop. Retro-Americana."

Brett grinned and looked somewhat relieved. "Right."

In the car Jessica searched for something to say. "What do you think of the Blues Hogs?" she asked.

"Blues Hogs?" Brett echoed. He wrinkled his forehead. Jessica waited, holding her breath. "Too derivative, you know?" he said finally.

"Oh, right," Jessica agreed. "There's nothing new about them."

Brett nodded and concentrated on his driving.

In her corner Jessica fidgeted with the bracelets on her arm. Apparently Brett was somewhat the silent type, just like Pierre. Maybe she should keep quiet, too, she decided. If Magenta was so cool she hardly ever spoke, that would certainly make an impression. Plus that way she wouldn't make any dumb mistakes. She gazed out the window with what she hoped was a suitably cool expression.

Her foot hit something on the floor. Looking down she saw a pile of cassette tapes. "What bands do you have?" she asked, starting to lean forward to pick some up.

"Here, let's listen to this," Brett cut in quickly. He grabbed a cassette off the dashboard and popped it into the player. The car was instantly flooded with raucous music.

Jessica gritted her teeth. "It's great!" she said over the noise. She liked rock, but she hated heavy metal, and this was definitely the latter. There was hardly even a melody.

Brett nodded.

Don't gush, Jessica told herself sternly. *Don't act like a teenybopper. Just be cool.*

Conversation was impossible for the rest of the ride because the music was so loud. Jessica tried not to act too relieved when they pulled into the parking lot of the Rock Spot. The only thing she worried about was that once they got inside the club the music would probably be even louder.

"Who's playing tonight?" Jessica asked as they headed for the door.

"X-Press," Brett said, sauntering beside her. He shrugged his broad shoulders inside his leather jacket. "Do you know them?"

Jessica searched her mind rapidly. It sounded vaguely familiar. "Sure. They're pretty hot."

Jessica had never been to the Rock Spot before. It was outside Sweet Valley, and none of her friends went there. But she didn't want Brett to find that out. She knew if she got to the door first and didn't know the routine, that would be a dead giveaway. As a delaying tactic, she stopped to extract an imaginary pebble from her shoe while Brett went ahead of her. When she caught up, he was just paying the cover charge.

The dance floor was crowded with bodies, and Jessica felt a little more at home. She was a good dancer and could always pick up any new steps quickly. She followed Brett to a table.

"Look at them," Brett said, nodding his head toward the dancers.

Jessica held her breath. Didn't he like to dance? His tone of voice wasn't very encouraging.

"I come for the music," Brett went on. He had to shout above the band. "How can you listen when you're jumping around?" His dark brown hair fell across his forehead in a way that made Jessica want to brush it back and put her arms around his neck.

"I know what you mean," Jessica shouted back as casually as it was possible to shout.

She didn't know if she was disappointed or relieved about not dancing—or about not talking, since it was obvious they wouldn't be able to do that, either. X-Press was so loud that Jessica could hardly hear herself think. But she was content just to catch Brett's eye now and then, and exchange a nod or a wry smile. He was concentrating hard on the music, so she pretended she was doing the same.

Once they left, she decided, they could get a little better acquainted. For the time being, though, Magenta was going to listen to the music and enjoy it, even if Jessica had to go deaf doing it!

*　　*　　*

When Jessica got home at midnight, she stopped by her twin's room to wave hello.

"How was it?" Elizabeth asked.

"What?" Jessica shouted back. She put one hand over one ear. There was a steady ringing inside her head that wouldn't go away.

"I said, how was it?" Elizabeth repeated in a slightly louder voice.

Jessica shrugged out of her leather jacket. "It was great," she said, trying to sound enthusiastic.

"What was the Rock Spot like?" her twin went on. "Does he go there a lot?"

Still cupping her ear, Jessica sat down on Elizabeth's bed. She frowned. "Well, I'm not sure," she yelled. "He didn't seem to know where the bathrooms were. But I guess he goes to the really cool places in L.A. all the time."

"Are you all right?" Elizabeth asked. "You're practically screaming! Are your ears OK?"

Jessica nodded. "Sure! It was fun! And he's such a hunk, too."

Elizabeth rolled her eyes, and Jessica stood up. Brett was definitely worth listening to a little loud music for. Still, Jessica couldn't help hoping that on their next date they could go somewhere quieter!

Seven

On Wednesday night "Daniella" was waiting for Pierre to pick her up. She hovered by the front door, ready to run out the instant he arrived.

"You look awfully pretty, Jess," her father said as he passed her in the hall. "I hope I didn't have to pay for that outfit, though."

"I borrowed it from a friend," Jessica explained. She glanced at her reflection in the hall mirror. The blue jacket and white linen skirt were two more items borrowed from Suzanne. Jessica hoped it was the right style for seeing a French film. She turned her head from side to side to admire her borrowed pearl stud earrings.

Just as she turned away from the mirror, she caught sight of something blue in her bangs.

Horrified, she leaned closer. One strand of hair was still dyed blue from Saturday night. She gritted her teeth and yanked the hair out.

"There's my date!" she said, hearing a car stop out front. With one last frenzied check of her bangs, she grabbed her bag and hurried out.

"*Bonjour*," she said as Pierre opened the car door for her.

Pierre smiled, showing his dimples. "*Bonjour*. I hope you like this film we're seeing. It's gotten great reviews in the European newspapers."

Jessica was impressed, but she tried not to show it.

"I've been wanting to see it ever since I first heard about it," she told him. It was the truth, too, since she first heard about it when Pierre invited her to go with him. But he didn't need to know that.

"I know I'll love it," she went on. "And I know you can help me out if there are a few French idioms I don't understand."

Pierre looked over at her. "It has subtitles, you know," he said, his blue eyes wide. "You won't need me to translate."

He's disappointed that I don't know more French, Jessica realized with a twinge of anxiety. On the spot, Jessica decided she had to act as though she understood every word of the movie.

I just hope they don't talk too fast! she thought.

But as soon as the movie started, she knew her hopes were in vain. The characters spoke so quickly she could only understand the simplest words and expressions, such as *oui* and *pardon, madame.* The subtitles didn't help, either, because the plot of the movie was so strange. As far as Jessica could tell, all the characters believed they were in purgatory, though to her it looked just like a doctor's waiting room. Every once in a while a nurse would call someone's name, and that person would look shocked and begin talking morosely about his childhood. Then the scene would switch to someone's apartment, and the characters would begin to talk about opera and the family's cheese-making factory. It didn't make any sense at all!

To make matters worse, every once in a while a little red ball would roll across whatever room the characters were in. No one in the film seemed to notice it. Jessica didn't have the slightest idea what it was supposed to symbolize, but she knew she had to have an opinion by the time the film was over. She darted a few glances at Pierre in the darkness. He was completely absorbed, his handsome profile highlighted by the screen's glow. Jessica wished she could relax and be herself with him, but she knew that was impossible.

By the time the lights came on, Jessica had a terrible headache.

"What did you think?" Pierre asked.

Jessica stood up, stalling for time by looking thoughtful. "Well, the image of the red ball was, uh, fascinating," she said hesitantly.

"Wasn't it?" he agreed. "It was really meaningful."

Jessica nodded. "And wasn't the camera angle unusual?" she said, her mind racing. She wasn't sure she could say anything about the plot without giving away the fact that she hadn't understood it. Talking about the technique seemed like a good diversion.

"Very," Pierre said. He offered his arm as they milled through the crowd. "It reminded me a lot of Ingrid Bergman's films."

Jessica frowned. Had she misunderstood him? Wasn't Ingrid Bergman an actress, and Ingmar Bergman the Swedish film director? Maybe Ingrid Bergman directed movies, too. She didn't want to make herself look dumb by asking, so she just nodded.

"Mmm," Jessica mumbled uncertainly. "I know what you mean."

Outside, a long line of people waiting to get

in snaked around the block. Jessica gazed at them absently, trying to come up with another subtle criticism to impress Pierre with. Just as she remembered a scene she could discuss, she saw someone on line who looked familiar. She looked away and followed Pierre down the sidewalk.

Then she glanced back at the line of people. The face she had seen looked like Brett's. But it must have been just a coincidence. French films were definitely not Brett's style. Studying so hard to be Daniella and Magenta meant she had both boys on her mind all the time, she realized. No wonder she was starting to see Brett in her imagination! Next time she went out with Brett she would probably imagine she saw Pierre slamdancing.

"Would you like some cappuccino?" Pierre asked her.

Jessica gave him a dazzling smile. If there was one thing she hated, it was coffee! "I'd love some," she said.

When Elizabeth reached the cafeteria on Thursday, she took a good look around.

"What are you waiting for?" asked Enid Rollins, who was standing right behind Elizabeth.

"I'm trying to decide where to sit." Elizabeth headed for a table by the wall.

"What? Wait!" Enid ran to catch up with her. Her green eyes looked puzzled. "We always sit over there," she said, pointing to a table in the middle of the lunchroom. It was crowded with their friends.

Elizabeth sat down. "So? Today I feel like sitting somewhere new."

Enid looked more baffled than ever. "But why? Are you upset about something?"

"No." Elizabeth's eyes twinkled. "I just want to get out of this rut I'm in. And you can help me," she went on eagerly.

Snapping open her soda, Enid said, "Sure. What is it?"

"Well. . . ." Now that Elizabeth had to say it, she felt embarrassed. She didn't know how her best friend would react to her new adventure campaign.

"What?" Enid prompted gently. She gave Elizabeth an encouraging smile.

Elizabeth smiled. "I want to be more spontaneous," she explained. "What do you think I could do to be more spontaneous?"

"First of all," Enid began, "you can't *plan* to be spontaneous. That's a contradiction in terms."

Elizabeth rolled her eyes. "See? That's exactly

my problem—I always have to plan everything so carefully before I do anything." She made a face. Obviously this course of action was long overdue!

"Are you really serious?" Enid asked.

Elizabeth nodded. "Very serious. And very *not* serious, too," she added mysteriously. "At least, I'm trying."

"I don't have the slightest idea what you're talking about," Enid admitted with a laugh. "But whatever it is, good luck."

Elizabeth smiled at her best friend. "Thanks. And don't be surprised if I do something that seems weird. It's all part of my plan."

Elizabeth knew she wasn't making much sense, but she didn't mind. After all, being sensible was exactly what she was trying to avoid!

On Thursday night Jessica had another blue streak in her hair. She wriggled into a blue strapless minidress and fastened a necklace of dice and tiddlywinks around her neck. In among the clicking pieces were Scrabble tiles that spelled out "Hard Rock."

"Where are you going tonight?" Elizabeth asked from the doorway.

Jessica pulled her hair up into a pony tail on the right side of her head. "Jax," she replied succinctly.

"Jax?" Her twin frowned. "Isn't that one of those places where people throw themselves off the stage into the crowd?"

With a shrug, Jessica turned up the collar of her jacket. "I don't know—maybe. Brett says the music is always on the cutting edge."

She caught her sister's eyes in the mirror and looked away. She didn't want to admit to Elizabeth that switching personalities from Daniella to Magenta was becoming a little exhausting! But she liked both boys, and she wasn't about to quit now. Besides, the dance was coming up in a week, and she still wasn't sure which boy she wanted to go with. After a couple more dates she would know.

"Maybe you should take ear plugs this time," Elizabeth suggested.

"Are you crazy?" Jessica asked. "Brett would think I was a big fake if I did that. No way."

"Well, just don't go jumping off any stages, OK?"

"I won't." Jessica was counting on the fact that Brett was too cool to dance. She hoped he was too cool to jump off stages, too.

But she also hoped he *wasn't* too cool to park

at Miller's Point later on. It was hard to cook up any romance when your eardrums were splitting!

She smiled at Elizabeth, then hurried out of the room.

Elizabeth was setting the table on Friday evening when the phone rang. Her mother picked up the receiver.

"Hello?" Mrs. Wakefield said. Her eyes widened in surprise. *"Who?"*

Elizabeth looked over. Her mother's expression was a picture of bewilderment.

"I'm afraid you have the wrong number. That's all right. Goodbye." Elizabeth's mother hung up the phone and let out a chuckle. "Well, that's a new one on me."

"Who was it?" Elizabeth asked.

Mrs. Wakefield went back to the stove. "Someone wanted to speak to a Magenta Galaxy," she replied. She laughed and shook her head. "That has to be the silliest name I ever heard."

"It sure is weird," Elizabeth agreed wholeheartedly. She put the plates down on the counter and added, "I'll be right back."

She slipped through the kitchen door and ran up the stairs. "Jess," she called out in a hoarse whisper. She peeked into her twin's bedroom. "Jessica?"

"I'm in the bathroom!" came her sister's voice.

Elizabeth went through the bedroom to the bathroom, where Jessica was busy trimming her split ends.

"You just missed a call from Brett," Elizabeth announced.

Jessica's face fell. "Darn! I didn't hear the phone ring! Who answered it?"

"Mom."

"Oh, no. What did she say to him?"

"She told him he had the wrong number," Elizabeth said. "What are you going to do? You can't answer the phone every time from now on just in case it's for Daniella or Magenta, you know."

"I know, I know," Jessica muttered. She picked up her hairbrush and began brushing her hair hard. "I'll have to figure out—" She snapped her fingers. "I know. I'll ask Lila."

While Elizabeth watched, Jessica ran back to her bedroom and grabbed the phone.

"Hi, Lila. It's me," Jessica said. "Could you do me a big favor?" She paused and stuck her tongue out at the phone. "I want to give Brett your phone number so he doesn't call me here anymore, OK? Then you can take messages and pass them on to me. Just say yes, Lila. Don't give me a hard time, please."

Elizabeth couldn't resist a laugh. Jessica and Lila were always involving each other in their crazy schemes. Their whole friendship seemed to be built on mutual plots and subterfuges.

"Great," Jessica said. "I'll talk to you later." She gave Elizabeth a thumbs-up sign. "All set. Now I have to tell Brett." She quickly dialed another phone number.

As Elizabeth wandered back downstairs, she heard her sister's Magenta voice leaving a message that she had a new phone number. Elizabeth shook her head. It was a miracle that Jessica's crazy plans didn't fall apart.

But of course there was still plenty of time for that to happen, Elizabeth realized. Even Jessica couldn't keep up such a masquerade forever.

Eight

Elizabeth lingered over breakfast on Saturday morning. She was almost at the end of *A Tale of Two Cities* by Charles Dickens, and she couldn't put it down. Finally, by ten o'clock she was finished.

"That was great." She stood and stretched as she looked over at her mother. "Jess should read it. I know she'd really like it."

"Speaking of Jessica, where is she?" Mrs. Wakefield asked. "Sleeping?"

Elizabeth grinned. "Remember, she needs her beauty sleep, Mom."

"At this rate she'll be the most beautiful girl in the world," Mrs. Wakefield said with a laugh.

As she trotted up the stairs to her bedroom,

Elizabeth thought about her plans for the day. As soon as she was dressed, she wanted to go to the mall to buy her dress. She was hoping her twin would want to come along.

She glanced into Jessica's room. "Jessica?" she whispered. There was no answer from underneath the shapeless mound of covers on the bed. "Jess?"

"Mmm-hmm."

"Do you want to go to the mall with me to buy that dress?" Elizabeth asked softly.

The lump on the bed wriggled slightly. "Mmm—what?"

Elizabeth tiptoed in. "Do you want to go to the mall with me?"

"Sure, Liz," Jessica mumbled. Then she flopped over again, sound asleep.

Elizabeth shook her head and went into the bathroom to take a shower. She knew that by the time she was ready to go, Jessica would suddenly decide she wanted to come along. Then she would have to take a twenty-minute shower, go through her morning ritual of trying on all her clothes, put on makeup, and finally eat breakfast! Elizabeth smiled to herself as she combed conditioner through her hair.

Jessica was still dead to the world by the time

Elizabeth was fully dressed. Elizabeth was standing in the doorway, contemplating her sister, when the phone rang. Jessica only twitched once at the sound, but Elizabeth hastily grabbed the extension by her twin's bed.

"Hello?" she answered.

"Hi, Daniella?" a boy's voice asked.

"No, just a moment, please." Elizabeth put her hand over the mouthpiece. "Jessica," she hissed, shaking her twin's shoulder. "It's Pierre."

Instantly Jessica sat bolt upright in bed. "What? Where?" she gasped.

"Here, it's Pierre," Elizabeth told her. She handed over the telephone.

Jessica cleared her throat, tossed her hair back, and put a sunny smile on her face. "Hi, Pierre," she murmured huskily into the receiver. "No, not at all. I was just reading the newspaper."

With a lopsided grin, Elizabeth headed back to the bathroom. "See you later," she mouthed.

"Dinner, tonight?" Jessica repeated. She looked at Elizabeth and waved goodbye. "That sounds wonderful. Six o'clock would be fine."

"How do you do it, Jess?" Elizabeth murmured. She shook her head, laughed, and went out the door.

*　　*　　*

Elizabeth walked slowly through the mall, looking at some of the displays. In front of Shear Glamour, a sign had been propped up that read: New Temporary Two-Week Perms! $20 Special Today!

Elizabeth stopped in her tracks and stared at the sign. Jessica wouldn't hesitate for a moment if she saw an offer like that. She would jump in feet first.

Elizabeth entered the salon. "Does the perm really only last for two weeks?" she asked one of the stylists, who was standing at the front counter.

"That's right," the stylist replied cheerfully. "It's like a test drive to see if you want a permanent perm. No appointment necessary," she added in an encouraging tone.

Elizabeth swallowed hard. The trick to being spontaneous was just to *do it*. "I'll do it," she said with grim determination.

"Are you sure?" the young woman said. She looked at Elizabeth a little apprehensively.

Elizabeth realized how grave and serious she had sounded, and let out a breathless laugh. Taking risks was scary, but it was fun, too! "Yes, I really want to," she said.

"OK," the stylist said. "Let's get started."

*　　*　　*

Lila heard the phone ring through a haze of sleep. She struggled awake and reached for the telephone. "Hello?" she croaked.

"Hi, can I speak to Magenta?"

Lila blinked sleepily. "Who? Oh, right," she corrected herself. She propped herself up on one elbow and rubbed her forehead. "Magenta isn't here right now, but I can take a message."

"Oh. This is Brett. Could you tell her that I got tickets to a concert tonight? If I don't hear from her, I'll just pick her up at six-fifteen so we can eat first. Got that?"

"Sure, no problem," Lila replied. She wondered if he was really as cute as Jessica said. He sure *sounded* cute. "I'll tell her—six fifteen."

"Great. Thanks a lot."

After Lila heard the dial tone, she punched in Jessica's phone number. She got a busy signal. Making a face, Lila hung up.

"Get off the phone, Wakefield," Lila muttered. She climbed out of bed and squinted at the clock. It was eleven-fifteen.

Now that she was awake, Lila was impatient to get going. She wanted to go to the mall and then to the beach. She hit the redial button on her phone, but the Wakefields' number was still busy.

"Come on," Lila grumbled. "I know it's you blabbing away, Jessica."

Glancing at her clock again, she decided to shower and then try Jessica one more time. If the line was still busy, she could call from the mall. And if the line was *still* busy, that was Jessica's problem. After all, Lila had only agreed to take messages, not spend her whole day trying to deliver them. If Jessica needed a secretary, she was welcome to hire one.

Lila took a long shower, tried on three outfits, and changed her shoes twice. When she was finally ready to leave, she called Jessica again. Still busy.

"Forget it, Jessica," Lila said testily as she slammed the receiver down. "I'm not waiting all day for you to get off the phone."

With an impatient sniff, Lila grabbed her bag and flounced out of her room. In minutes she was driving to the mall, looking forward to some serious shopping.

As usual, her first stop was Lisette's. The designer store almost always had something Lila wanted. At the sales desk she saw a familiar figure. Something about her was different, though. Then Lila let out a gasp.

"*Liz?*" she said in a shocked tone. She hurried to the counter and stared at her best friend's twin. "What did you do to your hair?"

Elizabeth spun around, her cheeks turning pink. "Hi, Lila. It's a two-week perm. What do you think?"

Elizabeth's hair was naturally wavy, but now it was positively curly, bobbing around her head like a golden halo.

Lila nodded slowly. "It's nice," she finally decided. "It's just so *different*, that's all."

"Good," Elizabeth said with a laugh. She ran her fingers through it. "That was the whole idea."

"Listen, can you give Jess a message?" Lila began. Then she noticed the dress Elizabeth was waiting to pay for. "Wow. That's nice," she said. She fingered the material appreciatively.

"Thanks," Elizabeth replied. "It's for the dance next weekend. Do you like it?"

Lila nodded. "I wonder why I didn't see this?" She shrugged. "Anyway, tell Jessica that Brett called this morning. He woke me up, too."

"Sorry," Elizabeth said, apologizing for her twin. "What's the message?"

"He said he has tickets to some concert, but he didn't say what. He'll pick her up at six-fifteen so they can eat first."

Elizabeth's eyebrows went up in an arch. "When?"

"Six-fifteen," Lila repeated.

"I mean what night?"

Lila started moving toward a rack of dresses. "Tonight," she called over her shoulder.

"Oh, no!"

Lila heard the note of dismay in Elizabeth's voice. She looked over. "What? What's wrong?"

Elizabeth shook her head, her new curls swaying back and forth. "She's going out with Pierre tonight," she said.

"So she can cancel one of them," Lila said airily. "What's the big deal?"

Elizabeth looked down at the dress on the counter. "I knew this would happen," she muttered. "I knew she would mess up somehow."

"Will that be cash or credit card?" the salesclerk asked.

Elizabeth held out a handful of bills. "I have a bad feeling about this," she said to Lila in a gloomy voice.

Lila gave Elizabeth a skeptical look. She didn't see what Elizabeth was getting so worked up about. Shrugging, she said, "It's her problem, not yours."

At that Elizabeth let out a short, sarcastic

laugh. "Lila, Jessica's problems always have a way of turning into my problems."

"That's true," Lila agreed. She smiled archly. "Well, have fun telling Jess the good news."

Then she turned and strolled out, leaving Elizabeth with an extremely worried look on her face.

Jessica was flipping through *The History of Art* with one hand while she waited for the nail polish on her other hand to dry. The book weighed a ton, and she couldn't keep her mind on the subject. But another date with Pierre meant another day of studying culture.

She sighed. Going out with someone as sophisticated as Pierre was a lot more work than she had expected. If he weren't so cute he wouldn't be worth it.

"Hi, Jess," Elizabeth said, coming in.

"*Liz!*" Jessica let out a screech and jumped off the bed. She ran to inspect her sister's hair. "I didn't know you were going to get a perm!"

"I didn't either," Elizabeth admitted. She grinned mischievously. "Do you like it?"

Jessica eyed her twin critically. "I'm not sure— it's just so different."

Elizabeth looked in the mirror and fluffed up her hair. "I know. I'm not sure if I like it or not. But at least it's only a temporary perm. If I decide I hate it, it'll only last two weeks."

"Way to go, Liz," Jessica said with admiration. "I'm proud of you."

Laughing, Elizabeth tossed her Lisette's bag onto the bed.

"Mission accomplished?" Jessica went on. "Did you get the dress?"

Her sister nodded and suddenly looked very serious. "Hey, Jess, I ran into Lila. She had a message for you from Brett."

"Great! What?" Jessica smiled happily, thinking of the good-looking rocker.

"You're not going to like it," Elizabeth said. "He's picking you up at six-fifteen tonight for dinner and a concert."

Jessica's mouth dropped open. *"What?"* she gasped. "I have a date with Pierre tonight!"

"Well, Lila didn't know that," Elizabeth pointed out as she headed for her room. "You could always call Brett and tell him you had other plans."

Jessica clenched her teeth. "But I don't have his phone number! I wrote it down, but now I can't find it! I already looked all over my room."

Elizabeth stopped in the doorway. "Do you have Pierre's phone number? Can you call him?"

Slowly Jessica shook her head. "Yes, but he told me he'd be out all day."

She let out a scream of frustration and flopped over backward on her bed. "It's all Lila's fault," she growled.

"What are you going to do?" Elizabeth asked.

Jessica closed her eyes. Her mind was racing. "I'll think of something," she said feverishly. "There has to be a way out of this."

Nine

Elizabeth opened up the shopping bag and carefully laid her new dress on her bed. From the other room she could hear Jessica slam the phone down.

"Aaagh!" Jessica screamed. "How could Lila do this to me?"

Shaking her head, Elizabeth clipped off the price tag and tried on the dress. She stood in front of the mirror, turning from side to side to watch the colors shimmer. She smiled happily, admiring the effect. Then she hunted through her closet to find her blue high-heeled sandals. When she had slipped them on, she took in the total effect again.

"You look great in that," Jessica announced from the doorway.

Elizabeth spun around, color brightening her cheeks. "Thanks," she said, looking in the mirror again. "I love this dress."

"Well, it's perfect for you. Aren't you glad you got it?"

Elizabeth let out a cheerful laugh. "Definitely. Thanks again for helping."

Her twin didn't speak for a few moments. At last the silence caught Elizabeth's attention. She looked at Jessica's expression in the mirror. Her sister had a look on her face that could only be described as scheming.

"What?" Elizabeth asked, growing suspicious. "What is it?"

Jessica crossed her arms. "I figured out what to do about tonight."

"That's good," Elizabeth replied. A little crease of uncertainty appeared in her forehead. "What are you going to do?"

"You mean, what are *we* going to do," Jessica corrected her.

Elizabeth whirled around to face her twin. "What are you talking about?" Her heart began pounding.

Jessica walked over and stood next to Elizabeth. Their identical images looked back at them from the mirror. "We've done it before," Jessica said softly.

"Oh, no, you don't! I'm not getting involved in one of your twisted plots." Elizabeth saw two bright spots of color appear on her cheeks. In the past the twins had traded places on critical occasions. Usually the occasions were critical to Jessica. And usually it was Elizabeth who ended up getting hurt or embarrassed or blamed.

Jessica lifted her chin stubbornly. "Didn't you say you owed me one?"

Elizabeth looked down at her new dress, then closed her eyes. She was doomed. "Jessica!" she moaned. "You know I'm going out with Todd tonight."

"You promised, Liz. I really need your help," Jessica insisted. "I can't cancel Brett and I can't cancel Pierre, but Todd would understand if you canceled. Then you could go out with Brett or Pierre tonight, pretending to be me."

"You mean pretending to be Daniella. Or Magenta," Elizabeth pointed out. She kicked off her sandals and crossed to the bed, where she slowly sank down. Having an identical twin had its advantages sometimes. But it also had its disadvantages, such as when Jessica wanted a double.

"It'll never work," Elizabeth began. "I don't know either one of them. How can I pretend I'm Magenta or Daniella?"

Jessica bit her lip. "Well, that's true. Um . . . I know! We'll take turns."

"What?" Elizabeth's eyes widened in shock. She shook her head vehemently. "What are you talking about?"

Full of enthusiasm, Jessica bounced over and sat down next to Elizabeth. "Listen, it's simple. We'll all go to the same restaurant, and every fifteen minutes or so, you and I can trade places. That way, I can keep talking about things I've already done with them. The guys will never know the difference."

Elizabeth gave her twin an incredulous look. "You've got to be kidding! We can't pull that off!"

"We *can*, Liz. Don't be such a pessimist." Jessica hugged her knees up to her chin. There was a frown of concentration on her face as she plotted out their strategy. "Here's how we'll do it. We'll wear the same basic outfit, black leotards and black skirts, but I'll start out with Magenta's jewelry and you can wear Daniella's accessories. And Suzanne's gray cropped jacket. And a beret," she added.

Elizabeth covered her face with her hands. She knew she was committed, whether she wanted to be or not. Sighing, she listened to Jessica outline the fiasco.

"I'll have to set my hair to be as curly as yours is now, and we'll each have a blue streak, but when we're being Daniella we can wear the beret to cover it up. This is a great idea!" Jessica said happily.

Elizabeth gave a bitter laugh. "Yeah, a great idea," she echoed. "Every fifteen minutes we go to the bathroom, where we change all our stuff and trade boys. What a brilliant plan." She looked up at her sister. "Jessica, it won't work. It's just a disaster waiting to happen."

"It is not," Jessica insisted. "It's the only way out."

Elizabeth arched her eyebrows. "There's always the option of telling the truth, you know."

Jessica brushed that suggestion aside with a wave of her hand. "Don't be ridiculous, Liz. This is what I want to do, and you promised to do whatever I asked. Besides, after tonight I'll know which one of them I like best, and I'll dump the other one."

Sighing, Elizabeth started to unzip her dress. "You're crazy, you know that?"

"No, I'm practical," Jessica retorted. She giggled. "Come on, Liz. It'll be fun!"

"*Fun?*" Elizabeth repeated in a sour voice. "That wasn't the word I was going to pick." But she nodded in resignation when Jessica gave her a beseeching look. "All right, all right. I'll do it."

She tried to ignore her misgivings. But she knew it was going to be tricky fooling both boys. Come to think of it, *impossible* was probably more like it.

"There he is! That's Pierre!" Jessica hissed. She gave Elizabeth a little shove. "Hurry up and get out of here before Brett shows up!"

Stumbling, Elizabeth pressed her beret down on her head and sent Jessica a dirty look. "All right. I'm going," she muttered.

Before she opened the front door, Elizabeth took a deep breath. To be fair to her twin, she had to give it her best effort, so she put a smile on her face and went outside to meet Pierre.

"Hi, Daniella," Pierre said as he walked up to the house.

"*Bonjour,*" Elizabeth replied. She kept smiling diligently.

"You look really nice," Pierre said, opening the car door for her. "That's a great beret."

"Thanks." Elizabeth knew her twin would appreciate the compliment. But dressing as Daniella made Elizabeth feel like a little girl playing dress-up. She felt ridiculous.

Jessica was right about one thing, though— Pierre was very good-looking. Elizabeth guessed that Jessica was attracted just by Pierre's looks alone.

"I have a big favor to ask," she added, just the way she and Jessica had rehearsed.

Pierre looked politely interested. "Yes?"

"Well, I don't know if you had something planned, but I really would love Chinese food tonight," Elizabeth explained. "Lotus House is very good."

Lotus House was also a big restaurant with two separate dining rooms. As long as Jessica and Elizabeth could maneuver their dates to opposite sides of the restaurant, they could pull off their masquerade. It was chancy, but then the whole operation was chancy. They had decided Lotus House was the least risky place to go.

"That sounds great," Pierre said. As he started the engine he added, "San Francisco has the best Chinese cuisine outside of the People's Republic, of course. That's where you get the most authentic cooking."

Elizabeth smiled, but privately she was offended. It was pretty snobbish to criticize the restaurant she had just asked to go to! She wondered if he was always like that, and if he was, how Jessica could like him.

"Well, I don't have time to go to San Francisco tonight," Elizabeth said dryly. She softened her words with a smile, though. "Lotus House is on Fremont Boulevard, just after the Bank of California."

"I go up to San Francisco pretty often," Pierre told her. "For the theater, exhibits, that sort of thing. When you can't be in Paris or New York, San Francisco is some compensation."

Snob, Elizabeth thought. *I'm not impressed.*

"That's nice," she said out loud.

Automatically, her hand came up to take off her beret. It was making her scalp itch. Just in time, however, she remembered the blue streak hidden underneath. Elizabeth pulled her hand back, sent evil thoughts out toward her twin, and gave Pierre another smile. The sooner this was all over the better.

"Here we are," Pierre said as they pulled into the Lotus House parking lot.

Elizabeth was silent as they were shown to a table. She already knew she didn't like Pierre very much. But when they sat down, she admitted to herself that she had to start keeping up her end of the bargain, no matter how much of a struggle it was.

"So," she began, "what was the last exhibit you saw in San Francisco?"

Pierre unfolded his napkin before he spoke. "It was—Greek pottery," he said.

"Really? I don't know very much about that," Elizabeth said truthfully. "Is there a particular style you like?"

A faint blush tinged Pierre's cheeks. "Well, of course. There's the, uh—"

Just then Elizabeth caught a glimpse of Jessica and her date standing in the main entrance. She moved her elbow and deliberately knocked her knife and spoon off the edge of the table.

"Oh!" she exclaimed.

Pierre held up one hand. "I'll get them." He bent down to pick them up. By the time he sat up again, Jessica and Brett had vanished into the other dining room.

"Thanks," Elizabeth said, breathing a sigh of relief. "So, you were telling me about Greek pottery?"

"Right." Pierre looked somewhat uncomfortable, in Elizabeth's opinion. He shifted his blue eyes to look over her shoulder and then glanced at the table. "It really wasn't a very good exhibition, actually. The best collection is at the Louvre, in Paris."

Elizabeth decided he was just name-dropping, something she couldn't stand. Pierre really was a first-class snob. Elizabeth couldn't understand what Jessica saw in him, aside from looks. But it wasn't her problem if her sister wanted to date him. All she had to do was talk to him without letting on that she wasn't who she said she was. Of course, Jessica wasn't who she said she was, either. It was all getting pretty convoluted!

"Do you spend much time in Paris?" she asked, trying to look interested. She opened her menu. At least she would get a nice Chinese dinner out of it.

"Mmm." Pierre nodded as he took a sip of water. "I love the Riviera. I spent most of my childhood there, and I go over as often as I can."

Elizabeth stared at him blankly. "Paris isn't on the Riviera."

"What?" Pierre let out an awkward laugh. "Oh, what I meant was, I spent most of my childhood going back and forth *between* Paris and the Riviera."

"Oh." Elizabeth smiled, but inwardly she was very skeptical. If she didn't know better, she would think Pierre didn't know what he was talking about.

Before she could say anything more, their waiter came. Elizabeth was glad for the interruption, since she was finding Pierre very difficult to talk to. There was something not quite right about him, but she wasn't sure what it was. With a mental shrug, she glanced down at the menu and ordered her favorite Chinese dish, ginger chicken.

"I was thinking about that movie we saw the other night," Pierre said a moment later. He cocked his head to one side. "I was wondering what you thought about that scene with the Ferris wheel."

Elizabeth felt her stomach jump. How could she fake that one? She didn't even know what the movie was called, let alone what to say about the scene he mentioned. All Jessica had told her about the movie was that it was "weird, confusing, and awful." Anxiously Elizabeth glanced at her watch.

"Oh, I have to make a phone call. Will you excuse me for a minute? I'll be right back," she said with a gasp.

Without waiting for an answer, she jumped out of her chair and headed for the ladies' room. It was time for the first switch!

Ten

Elizabeth paced back and forth in the ladies' room. She grumbled silently at her sister while she unclipped her earrings, pulled off the beret, and took off the jacket. She was sure this was the silliest, most idiotic escapade she had ever taken part in. Being adventurous was one thing. Making a fool out of yourself was another.

Jessica burst through the door and immediately began stripping off Magenta's accessories. "Hi, Liz. I saw you come in! It's working great!"

Elizabeth stared at Jessica. "Great? You call this great?" She started putting on Magenta's bracelets.

"Sure." Jessica laughed. She tucked her blue streak securely under the hat and shot Elizabeth a worried look. "You aren't messing up, are you?"

"No." Elizabeth grimaced while she fastened the bright necklace made of fluorescent fish around her throat. "What were you and Brett talking about, just so I know?"

Jessica examined her reflection in the mirror. "Oh, classic rock 'n' roll. The Beatles, you know. All those ancient bands."

Just then the ladies' room door swung open, and a petite Chinese woman walked in. Silently she took in the scene: two identical girls trading clothes in the bathroom. Nobody said a word for several seconds.

Then the woman smiled, nodded, and slipped into a stall without comment. Jessica met Elizabeth's eyes in the mirror and winked.

"Come on, hurry up," Jessica whispered.

Elizabeth held back a sigh. "By the way, just before I came in here Pierre was asking me about that movie you guys saw the other night. Something about a Ferris wheel?"

"Ferris wheel?" Jessica looked puzzled. Then she smiled. "Oh, right. I think it was a symbol of something. Maybe it was a symbol of the universe. Don't you think it could be?"

Elizabeth laughed. She felt as if she were starring in a madcap farce. And anyway, it seemed better to laugh about it than to scream, which was the alternative. "Whatever you say, Jess. Universe, man in the moon, apple pie. Whatever. Anything round."

"Oh, you're right," Jessica agreed, frowning. "Maybe it's something about the cycle of life. You know, birth, life, death, rebirth—"

Elizabeth steered her sister toward the door and pushed her out. "See you in fifteen minutes."

As Elizabeth made her way through the other dining room, she summoned up everything she knew about classic rock 'n' roll. In a corner booth she caught sight of the boy who had come in with Jessica. Squaring her shoulders, she headed for him. He had to be Brett. He was attractive, too, with a tousled, bad-boy look, but for some reason he seemed a little uncomfortable, even out of place. Elizabeth wondered if he disliked Chinese restaurants.

"I'm back," she announced, sliding into the booth seat opposite him.

Brett nodded. "Great."

Elizabeth nodded, too. She didn't know what to say. After all, she had never seen him before, but she had to pretend otherwise. This was a little awkward, to say the least!

"So," she began. She looked at the table. There wasn't any food, and she didn't know whether Jessica and Brett had ordered already. "I'm starved," she said truthfully.

"Me, too," Brett agreed. He craned his neck looking for a waiter. "Any day now, we might be able to order," he observed wryly.

Elizabeth smiled, wondering what to say next. "Do you have a lot of old albums?" she asked finally.

Brett nodded. "Yeah, sure."

"Oh." Elizabeth toyed with her fork. Brett was a little hard to converse with, too. "What's your favorite old band?"

"Rolling Stones, the Doors, those guys," Brett answered. He gave her a lopsided smile and then looked away.

Elizabeth kept expecting him to keep the conversational ball rolling, but he didn't. She sighed and tried again.

"I like the Stones, too," she said. "I think the real test of a band's music is if it still sounds good years later, you know?"

"Definitely," Brett agreed. He looked up with obvious relief when the waiter appeared. "Great, we can order. It's about time."

Elizabeth ordered ginger chicken again. She knew she would be switching places with Jessica every fifteen minutes, and this way she would be sure to have ginger chicken wherever she was. Brett ordered sweet and sour pork, which she thought was pretty unadventurous.

When they were alone again, Brett leaned back in his chair. "The Doors are the same way—like you were just saying. Their music is still great after twenty years. Take—oh—" He broke off, searching for an example. " 'Sympathy for the Devil,' for instance."

Elizabeth blinked. "Isn't that a Rolling Stones song?" she asked bluntly.

"Oh! Yeah, I meant that's an example of a great *Stones* tune," Brett corrected himself. His face turned pink, and instead of meeting her eyes, he stared glumly at his water glass.

"Right," Elizabeth said, frowning in confusion. *What's going on?* she wondered. *First Pierre thinks Paris is on the Riviera, and now Brett mixes up classic songs even I know about!*

An awkward silence descended on the table. Elizabeth was getting fed up with the evening. Brett could hardly answer more than a simple yes or no to anything Elizabeth said. And the alternative was just as bad. In a few moments it would be time to go back to Pierre the Pompous. Elizabeth scowled at her watch.

"Listen," Brett began suddenly. He sat forward in his chair, an anxious look on his face. "I have to tell you—"

"One ginger chicken, one sweet and sour pork," the waiter interrupted as he set their plates down in front of them.

"Oh—" Brett looked startled.

Elizabeth stood up abruptly. "I'll be right back. I want to—" She broke off, wondering what excuse she could give that would sound reasonable. Then she realized she no longer cared if she sounded reasonable. "I'll be right back."

She strode off toward the ladies' room again. She was ready to call the whole thing off, deal or no deal.

Jessica got to the bathroom first. She was taking off Daniella's earrings when her twin stormed in.

"I've had it," Elizabeth announced. "This has gone too far, Jess. I'm really sick of it."

Jessica stared at her sister. "Liz! You can't! Don't ruin it for me!"

"I mean it, Jessica." Elizabeth kicked off Magenta's high-heeled shoes. "Both of these guys are total morons. I don't know how you can like either one of them."

A wave of panic swept over Jessica. If Elizabeth walked out on her, she would lose both boys at once! She grabbed Elizabeth's hand. "Liz! Please! You promised me!"

For a moment, they stared at each other. Jessica could tell her twin was about to abandon the whole project. Tears sprang to her eyes.

"Liz, I've worked so hard! I really need you!" She squeezed her twin's hand. If guilt failed, there was always plain begging. "Please!"

Elizabeth closed her eyes. "Oh, Jessica! This is so stupid and embarrassing. I really hate it." Her voice had lost its angry edge, however, and Jessica knew she had won.

"I know, but it's really important to me," Jessica insisted. She unfastened the necklace from around Elizabeth's throat. "After this I won't ever ask you for another thing in our entire lives."

"Yeah, right," Elizabeth said. "Don't make empty promises, Jess." She put the beret on her head, though.

Jessica heaved a sigh of relief. "You're the best, Liz. What were you and Brett talking about?"

"Nothing," Elizabeth said tersely. "Absolutely nothing."

Jessica gave her sister a doubtful look. "Well, hurry up. Daniella wouldn't keep Pierre waiting too long." When Elizabeth glared at her, Jessica ducked out the door.

"Hi," she gasped, plopping down across from Brett again. She wondered nervously if Elizabeth would keep playing the part. More than anything she wished she could be in two places at once. She didn't want Elizabeth to spoil things for her. "Hey, the food came. Great."

As she lifted her fork to her mouth, Jessica nearly let out a yelp of horror. On her wrist was the delicate watch she had borrowed from Suzanne! Magenta would *never* wear anything so conservative. For that matter, neither would *she*. She hated watches.

"Hey! Look over there!" she commanded in a strangled voice.

Brett twisted around to look over his shoulder, and Jessica fumbled to get the watch off her wrist. By the time he turned around again she had stuffed it in her pocket, but her heart was pounding like crazy.

"What was it?" Brett asked. He had a puzzled look in his dark-brown eyes.

"I thought it was the lead singer from that band, Rotten Apples, but I guess not," Jessica mumbled.

Quickly she put a big forkful of dinner in her mouth and nearly gagged. Her twin had ordered chicken with ginger, a spice Jessica loathed. Trying not to shudder, she chewed and swallowed. Why couldn't Elizabeth have ordered something normal like moo shu pork?

"How is it?" Brett asked.

Jessica gave him a weak smile. "Great. It's really good."

She stuffed another heaping forkful into her mouth. While she chewed, she stared off into the distance. She was trying to keep a straight face and not grimace. Gradually she realized she was staring at an old lady, who was giving her a very indignant look in return. Brett was completely silent.

"Don't you just hate the way people stare at you when you're the least bit different?" Jessica asked when she remembered to be Magenta again. "As if everybody has to conform to one way of dressing and acting."

Brett nodded without looking up. "Right."

"Just because I want to make a statement about who I am," Jessica chattered on. Between worrying about Elizabeth and Pierre, keeping an eye on the time, and struggling through the ginger chicken, Jessica was barely paying attention to Brett. She was feeling a little bit out of control. She drew a deep breath so she could keep talking.

"Magenta," Brett cut in.

Jessica looked up at him. "What?"

He pushed some food around on his plate. He had eaten almost nothing. "Magenta, I really think we need to talk about something."

"Like what?" Jessica pulled the watch out of her miniskirt pocket and glanced at it. It was time to switch! "Oh! Hey, I just remembered something," she gasped. She dropped her fork on her plate and jumped up.

Brett stared at her in surprise. "Are you going to the ladies' room *again*?"

Color flared in Jessica's cheeks. "Yeah. It's kind of personal," she said. "Do you mind?"

She dodged her way among the tables again, nearly bumping into a busboy. Feeling frazzled, she burst into the ladies' room.

Elizabeth was already there, stripping off Daniella's accessories. "That's it!" Elizabeth fumed as soon as she saw Jessica. "This is the most humiliating thing I've ever done in my life!"

Jessica stared at her sister. Everything was falling to pieces! If Elizabeth walked out now, Jessica would have to make a choice between Pierre and Brett instantly. And she didn't know which one she should pick!

"Listen," Elizabeth continued. She faced Jessica squarely. "I think Pierre is a big fake, and I told him so. He's never been to France in his life. He's just making everything up to sound interesting."

Jessica's jaw dropped. "You *what*?"

Elizabeth was beginning to cool down. She shook her head. "I'm sorry, Jess. I just couldn't stand listening to him anymore. I know more about art history and classical music than he does."

"I can't believe you did that!" Jessica squashed the beret down on her head and gave her sister an outraged glare. "I'll just apologize, that's all. Here, give me those," she growled, pushing Elizabeth aside and stepping into Daniella's conservative pumps.

Elizabeth was slowly turning into Magenta again, but there was a grim, set look to her jaw that Jessica knew well. It took a lot to make Elizabeth angry, but when she reached her limit, everyone around her knew it!

"If you've ruined this whole thing, I'll really be mad," Jessica said defensively. Giving her twin another icy look, she stalked out of the bathroom.

"Hi, I'm back," she told Pierre. She smiled angelically at him. "I'm sorry about that. I don't know what came over me just then."

Pierre was staring down at his plate, pushing

snow peas around with his fork. He shook his head. "No, don't apologize," he said in a gloomy tone. He looked sad and dejected. "You were right."

"Don't be silly," Jessica insisted.

Pierre just shook his head again, not saying anything.

Jessica slumped in her chair. It was hopeless now. Whatever Elizabeth had said to him had done irreparable damage. It looked as though she had lost Pierre.

"Maybe I should just take you home," Pierre mumbled. His suave, sophisticated manner had evaporated.

"Yeah, I guess." Jessica tossed her napkin onto the table and folded her arms. It was no use trying any more. Elizabeth had ruined her chances with Pierre.

Well, there was still Brett, as long as Elizabeth didn't spoil things with him, too.

Eleven

When Elizabeth got home she heard Jessica banging around in the bathroom. She threw herself facedown on her bed, and behind her she heard the bathroom door fly open.

"I don't want to talk about it!" she announced into her pillow.

"*You* don't?! What about me?" Jessica cried. "You completely ruined this whole thing!"

Elizabeth sat up to return her sister's exasperated look. "Well, you completely humiliated me, Jessica. I knew it would be a disaster, and it was. I told you at the beginning what a dumb idea it was to go out with both of them, and now it's all fallen apart on you."

"Whose fault is that?" Jessica paced angrily

back and forth. Her blue-green eyes were stormy. "Who asked you to insult Pierre?"

Exhausted, Elizabeth closed her eyes. "Jessica, he was a fake. I told him the truth, that's all."

"Great. And did you manage to insult Brett, too?" Jessica snapped. "I notice you didn't go to the concert with him."

Elizabeth kicked off her shoes and sent Jessica a defiant look. "As a matter of fact, I thought he was a big fake, too. I told him I didn't want to go to the concert or anywhere else with him."

Jessica gasped. "Oh, great! Just great! Now neither one of them will ever want to see me again!"

"Both of them were total jerks," Elizabeth said. "You're better off without them." She rubbed her forehead. Her head ached, she was hungry, and she hated fighting with her twin. The whole evening had been a nightmare.

Jessica was staring at her with an open mouth and an expression of utter astonishment. "Who gave *you* the right to decide? Maybe I really liked them! But you decided I shouldn't go out with them. Thanks a lot, big sister!" Jessica stormed out, slamming the door behind her.

Elizabeth sighed. How many times had Jessica taken other people's romances into her own hands? How many times had she decided that certain couples should be split up or forced together? Elizabeth had lost track.

But of course that didn't make it right for her to do it to Jessica. Just because she thought Pierre and Brett were idiots didn't mean she had the right to tell them so on Jessica's behalf.

"Oh, *yuck!*" Elizabeth groaned, lying on her bed again. She didn't want to think about it anymore. From beginning to end, switching roles had been a miserable experience, and the sooner she forgot about it the happier she would be.

But the following morning thoughts of what she had done the evening before weighed heavily on her conscience. Now that the humiliation had worn off, Elizabeth was beginning to feel guilty.

I should really do something to fix it, she thought.

From the bathroom came a series of banging and slamming noises that told Elizabeth her twin was still very angry with her.

"Jess?" Elizabeth called out. Her tone was apologetic. She was regretting everything she had said the night before, especially to her sister.

There was no reply. "Jessica?" Elizabeth called again.

Then she heard a door slam and feet passing her bedroom. Jessica was gone.

Elizabeth let her breath out slowly. She didn't know what she could do to repair the damage. If only she could call Pierre and Brett and explain things! But Jessica only had Pierre's number, not Brett's. There had to be a way to reach them both and sort everything out.

The answer came after Elizabeth had finished her breakfast, when Lila called with a message for Jessica.

"Brett called this morning and woke me up again," Lila grumbled. "Doesn't he know it's Sunday? Normal people like to sleep—"

"What did he say?" Elizabeth cut in hopefully.

Lila yawned into the phone. "He left his number this time so Jess—I mean *Magenta*—can call him back."

Elizabeth's eyes lit up. "Great! That's just what I need," she exclaimed. "Thanks a lot!"

Once she had Brett's phone number, she knew just what to do.

Jessica bounced her tennis racket on the heel of her hand. "Ready to be massacred?" she called out.

Across the court, Cara Walker let out a fake screech. "Have mercy, please!"

"No way," Jessica announced. Then she tossed up a tennis ball and smashed it across the net.

"Hey!" Cara swiped at it wildly, flipped her racket into the air, and jumped out of the way. "Are you trying to kill me?" she gasped.

Jessica gave her friend a sweet smile. Playing tennis under the influence of raging anger was always lethal—for her opponent. She waggled her eyebrows up and down. "Just get your racket back, Cara."

For the next thirty minutes, Jessica blew off steam by taking it out on the tennis ball. Poor Cara was beginning to look frantic, but Jessica didn't slow down. After a while, though, she noticed a cute boy beyond the fence, watching her play.

Flattered, Jessica swung around for a two-handed backhand. That gave her the chance to get a closer look at him. He smiled at her.

Jessica pretended not to notice. "Time out!" she called to Cara after winning the point. She jogged toward the net and grabbed her towel.

"What's up?" Cara asked, joining her.

Jessica met her friend's dark eyes. "Do you see that cute guy over there?" she asked, wiping her forehead. "He's been watching me."

Cara glanced over Jessica's shoulder. She

125

grinned. "He *is* a hunk. And he's definitely watching you."

"I'm going to get a drink, OK?" Jessica said.

Their eyes met, and they both giggled. The cute boy was standing right next to the water fountain.

"Sure, I bet you're really thirsty," Cara replied in an innocent tone.

"Parched," Jessica shot back airily. She laced her fingers through her racket strings and began strolling toward the gate, pretending she was fixing the strings.

"Excuse me," she said as she reached the water fountain.

"Sure." The boy was about four inches taller than she was, with straight blond hair and a dimple in his chin. He was dressed for tennis, too, and his shorts showed off his muscular legs.

"You're pretty ferocious," he observed, grinning while Jessica was taking a drink.

"For a *girl*?" Jessica retorted in a challenging tone. She licked a drop of water off her lower lip.

He grinned. "No—for anybody. We should get together and play sometime. My name's Tony Mangino."

"I'm Jessica Wakefield," she said. She gave

126

him a friendly smile. It was nice to use her real name for a change. She glanced back to the court at Cara.

"Oh, if your friend—" Tony began.

"There's no rush," Jessica said. "Let's definitely get together sometime. For tennis," she added with a flirtatious grin.

Tony's blue eyes twinkled. "Or even basketball."

"Right." Jessica laughed.

She loved being free and easy with boys. After all the nervous studying she had done for Pierre and Brett, she found it relaxing and fun to talk to Tony and just be herself. And now that she thought about it, maybe her sister really had done her a favor. At first she had been furious with Elizabeth, but the idea of not having to become Magenta or Daniella again was a big relief.

Who needs them? Jessica asked herself. *I hate cappuccino, and I got split ends from washing that blue gunk out of my hair so often.*

"Coming back, Jessica?" Cara called out in a teasing voice.

Jessica looked over at her friend and stuck out her tongue. "I guess I have to go," she told Tony, starting to walk away. "Why don't you call me sometime?"

"Great. Why don't you give me your phone number?" Tony said.

Jessica laughed at her forgetfulness. "Oh, right." She gave him her number, then jogged back onto the court.

"Did he ask you out?" Cara whispered when Jessica reached her.

Jessica arched her eyebrows. "What do you think?"

"You're a real pro," Cara declared. "Let's go to the Dairi Burger and have lunch. I'm starved."

On the way to the popular burger hangout, Jessica filled Cara in on the previous night's fiasco. "What a joke," she moaned. "Brett and Pierre must've thought I had some kind of disease, the way I had to keep going to the bathroom."

Cara hooted with laughter as she pulled into the parking lot. "I guess you aren't going out with either one of them anymore, huh?" she said.

"No way." Jessica rolled her eyes. "They were too much work!"

When they got inside, Jessica spotted Dana Larson sitting in a booth with some other people. Jessica hid her face with her hand. "Oh, no," she muttered.

Cara's eyes widened. "What's wrong?"

"Dana's over there," Jessica whispered. "I

don't feel like taking all her stuff back today. I don't want her to see me."

"Yeah, well, it's too late. She's coming over," Cara said in a soft voice.

Jessica sighed and turned around. "Hi, Dana," she said.

"Hey, Jessica," Dana greeted her. She had two New York City subway tokens dangling from her ears. "How's the studying going?"

Jessica grimaced. "Well, I'm not actually going out with that guy anymore."

"Great. I really need some of that stuff I loaned you."

Jessica smiled innocently. "I'd be happy to drop it all off at your house this afternoon, but I have to get home because I'm expecting a call from my grandmother, who's in the hospital," she lied. The truth was that she was just too lazy to pack it all up and drive to Dana's. "If you wanted to stop off, though, that would be OK."

"Sure," Dana agreed. "I need it, so I'll drop by a little later."

Jessica smiled again. "See you later." Then she went to the pay phone and dialed Suzanne's number. She told Suzanne the same sob story about waiting for her grandmother to call, and

Suzanne said she would pick up her things on her way to an exhibit that afternoon.

"That's all taken care of," Jessica said with satisfaction as she got back on line. Cara was all the way up to the counter, so Jessica was able to order her lunch without having to wait at all.

"Your timing is perfect, Jessica," Cara said cynically.

Jessica picked up her soda and lifted it in the air for a toast. "I know, Cara. I know."

Elizabeth peeked from behind the curtain in the living room again. *I wonder if I did the right thing*, she wondered, scanning the street. *I'll really have to wing it if Jess doesn't come back soon.*

If her solution to last night's fiasco was going to work, Jessica needed fair warning about what Elizabeth had done. But if Jessica didn't show up . . .

Just then her twin drove up to the house and hopped out of the car. She swung her tennis racket over her shoulder and actually *skipped* to the door. She looked lighter than air. Puzzled, Elizabeth met her in the hall.

"Hey, Liz," Jessica said in a carefree voice. She hummed and checked her appearance in the hall mirror. "Isn't it a great day?"

Elizabeth knew Jessica had dramatic shifts in mood, but this was amazing. Just hours before, Jessica had left the house in an indignant huff, and now she was floating on air.

"What's gotten into you?" Elizabeth asked.

Jessica grinned. "Wouldn't you like to know!"

Elizabeth shook her head. "Listen, I have to tell you something, Jess—"

"Can't it wait, Liz?" Jessica interrupted. "I'm dying of thirst." For some reason this made her smile.

Elizabeth frowned. "Well, it's pretty import-ant—"

The door bell cut her off.

"That's probably Suzanne or Dana," Jessica announced, heading for the door. "They're sup-posed to stop by and pick up all their junk."

With one frantic look at her twin, Elizabeth ran for the stairs. She had to stay out of sight. Standing on the first step, she heard the front door open.

"Pierre!" Jessica croaked. "What—what are you doing here?"

Elizabeth winced. So much for warning Jessica!

Twelve

Jessica gaped at Pierre. Without her Daniella facade on, she felt as though he had caught her red-handed at something embarrassing.

Pierre cleared his throat. "Daniella, I'm really glad you called—"

For the moment, Jessica was too flustered to be puzzled. "Come in," she said, leading the way into the living room. She sank down into a chair. She crossed and recrossed her legs, wondering if he would realize she wasn't really Daniella at all.

"Daniella—"

"I called you?" Jessica cut in. She heard footsteps run upstairs, and she realized what had happened: Elizabeth. Her twin was trying to fix things. Well, now Jessica was in a fix, all right.

"I wanted to tell—"

"Hang on," she ordered brusquely.

She dashed out of the room, leaving Pierre in mid-sentence.

"Liz!" Jessica whispered up the stairs. There was total silence. Jessica scowled. "Thanks a lot," she muttered.

Still scowling, Jessica went back into the living room. Pierre took one look at her face and blushed to the roots of his hair.

"I know what you're thinking, and I don't blame you," he said.

Jessica took a good look at him for the first time since he had appeared. "Hey, wait a second," she began. "You look different."

It was true. Instead of the preppy, polished Pierre she was used to, she was seeing a more slick, trendy version. Pierre's light brown hair was combed back differently, and he was wearing black jeans and a T-shirt instead of khakis and an oxford-cloth shirt.

"That's what I was trying to tell you," Pierre explained. He looked very sheepish. "You were right last night when you called me a fake. I am—or I was—or *Pierre* was," he faltered.

Jessica blinked. She was completely taken aback. "Pierre was?" she repeated.

Blushing, Pierre said, "My real name is Pete.

Pete Lake. And I'm not like that at all—not like Pierre. I don't like classical music very much, and I've never been to France. I read all that stuff in books, and a lot of it I just made up to impress you."

"To impress me?" Jessica knew she was echoing everything he said like a parrot. But she was so startled, she couldn't think. "But why?" she finally asked.

Pete shrugged. "I wanted to meet a different kind of girl from the type I usually date. I wanted to meet someone more sophisticated—like you," he confessed.

A surprised laugh bubbled up inside Jessica. He had been faking the cultured-world-traveler act all along, too! It was pretty funny. Jessica started shaking her head in amazement.

"I know," Pete continued in a rush. He stood up and began pacing back and forth. "I know it's stupid. I just didn't realize I would make such a fool of myself. I should have known I couldn't fake it with someone like you, Daniella. I'm really sorry."

"Listen—" Jessica began.

The door bell cut her off. Letting out a deep breath, Jessica said, "Hang on a second. Some friends are coming over to pick up some stuff."

Jessica walked slowly to the front door, thinking over the ironic turn of events. Giggling, she yanked the door open.

Then her heart started galloping. "Brett!" she gasped. She was thunderstruck. Elizabeth had really fixed things now!

Brett was standing on the front step, looking anxious. "Magenta, hi. Thanks for asking me over."

"Sure, no problem," Jessica said in a dazed voice. "Come on in."

She put a silent curse on her twin sister. If this was Elizabeth's idea of making up for last night, she had some pretty strange notions. How could Elizabeth do this to her? Now she had to juggle both boys at once, with no one to cover for her. It was terrible!

With a sigh Jessica took Brett to the den. She was wondering frantically how long she could keep Pierre waiting and how she would be able to keep them separated. What an embarrassing predicament.

"Magenta, I wanted to tell you last night, but I didn't have the nerve—" Brett began.

Jessica looked at him with narrowed eyes. "Hey, you look different," she said. "You look like you're going boating or something," she concluded.

"I know." Brett dug his hands into the pockets of his chinos. With them he was wearing a bright blue polo shirt and brown boat shoes. He gave her a guilty smile. "This is what I usually look like," he admitted. "I was pretending to be the kind of rock 'n' roller you like—but I didn't know what I was doing."

"Don't tell me—" Jessica clapped one hand to her forehead. "You wanted to meet a different kind of girl, so you put on this big act."

Brett nodded, his dark eyes wide. "That's right! How did you know?" Then he shook his head and let out a disgusted snort. "I should have known you would see through me. It was stupid to think I could fool you. A girl like you—you're too smart to fall for such a dumb stunt."

"Oh, no." Jessica sank back in her father's desk chair and shook her head. "I don't believe this."

"But it's not what you think," Brett cut in quickly. "I really like you! I wasn't trying to hide anything. I just wanted to be somebody different for once."

Jessica glanced up at him, remembering something that had puzzled her a few nights earlier. "Hey, were you at the Odeon the other night for that weird French movie?"

Brett's eyes lit up. "Yes! I thought it was

really interesting. Were you there?" he asked, sounding surprised.

"Sort of," Jessica answered. She looked over at the door. She had to get back to Pierre—Pete—pretty soon. She was ready to kill her twin. It was all Elizabeth's fault for getting her into this mess.

"Look, can you wait here a second?" she asked, springing up. She shut the door firmly and headed back to the living room.

And then the door bell rang again.

"No!" Jessica groaned. "Who could it be *now*?" she said in an exasperated voice. Spinning on her heel, she lunged for the front door again.

Dana and Suzanne were both on the doorstep.

"Hi," Dana said breezily. "We pulled up at the same time."

Suzanne gave Dana a haughty look. "Just by chance," she added. Obviously Suzanne didn't want anyone to think she would go anywhere deliberately with someone as funky as Dana.

Jessica looked at them both. Now she had to return their things without letting either one of them know about the *other* pile of borrowed items. How could she explain that she had been using both of them? And on top of that, she still had to sort things out with Pierre and Brett. Or Pete and Brett. Or Pete and whoever, if Brett wasn't really Brett's name. . . .

Suddenly Jessica decided she had had enough. "Come on in," she said, turning away. "I'll be right back."

Leaving them both in the hallway, Jessica ran up the stairs.

"Elizabeth Wakefield!" she yelled, bursting into her twin's room.

Elizabeth was sitting at her desk. "How's it going?" she asked in a hopeful tone.

"How's it going?" Jessica said. Her voice rose. "How's it *going*? It's going terribly! Who asked you to invite those guys over?"

Elizabeth looked pained. "I thought it would help," she explained. "I felt so bad about last night—"

"Great!" Jessica said. She threw her hands up in the air. "First you make a big mess last night, then you make it even bigger today!"

"I was only trying to help," Elizabeth retorted. "I'm sorry if it isn't going very well. I thought you would appreciate a chance to work things out with them."

Jessica let out a sarcastic laugh. "Work things out? I can't even get a word in edgewise, they're both talking so fast about how sorry they are about faking who they were."

"What?" Elizabeth's eyebrows flew up in surprise.

"Right," Jessica said. She flung herself down into a chair. "How do you like that? The nerve of those guys, trying to pretend to be something they're not! Well, forget it. I'm not wasting any more time on them."

Elizabeth was shaking her head. "Whoa! Hang on a second. You mean they were *both* faking it, too? Just like you were?"

Jessica felt a guilty blush heat up her cheeks. "Well, it's not exactly the same," she faltered.

"It's not?" Elizabeth was beginning to grin. "Exactly how is it different?"

"It's—I was really—" Jessica struggled for words. She met her sister's gaze and started to laugh. "This is pretty dumb, huh?"

Elizabeth chuckled. "You three were made for one another!"

Rolling her eyes, Jessica said, "No, I don't think so. I've had it with both of them."

"Are you going to tell them you were faking it, too?" Elizabeth asked.

Jessica shrugged. "Well, maybe. I met someone new at the tennis courts today, and I like him a lot better. I don't really care what those guys think any more."

"It's better to start from scratch, right?" Elizabeth said.

"Right," Jessica agreed, smiling crookedly.

Then she clapped one hand over her mouth. "Wow, I almost forgot. Dana and Suzanne are here, too. I have to give them back all their stuff."

"I'll help," Elizabeth offered, standing. "Why don't you go downstairs and explain what's taking so long, and I'll start packing up all their things."

Jessica jumped up and gave her sister a hug. "Thanks, Liz. See you in a minute." Grinning, she hurried downstairs. But when she got to the bottom of the stairs, Dana and Suzanne were no longer there. Jessica frowned and peeked into the den. It was empty, too. Brett was gone. With growing confusion, she hurried into the living room. No Peter. There was no sign of anyone.

"What's going on here?" Jessica muttered.

Puzzled, she walked through the dining room toward the kitchen. And then she stopped. Through the sliding glass door of the dining room, she could see the backyard.

On the patio, two couples were deep in conversation. Dana and Pete were sitting together, nodding and gesturing, and nearby, Suzanne and Brett were talking earnestly, too. None of them was aware of her watching them from the house.

"I can't believe this," Jessica said out loud. Then she laughed. It looked as though computer dating worked after all!

"Hey, you guys," she said, sliding the door open.

All four of them looked her way. Each of them wore a funny mix of expressions—confusion, surprise, and excitement.

"Is your name Jessica?" Pete asked in a perplexed tone.

Brett frowned. "I thought it was Magenta."

"*Magenta*?" Dana echoed. She laughed and arched one eyebrow at Jessica.

"*I* thought it was Daniella," Pete said. "I don't get it."

Jessica felt a blush heat her cheeks, but she knew the only way out was to bluff it. "Just an idea I had," she explained, sinking into a chair. She sent one of her most dazzling smiles to Brett and Pete. "No offense."

"Sure," Brett said slowly. Then he glanced at Suzanne, and a look of happiness spread across his features. "No problem. I was just talking to Suzanne—we have a lot in common."

"I hope you don't mind," Suzanne broke in. "I thought it would be all right to help myself to a glass of water, and then Brett came into the kitchen and we just started talking."

142

"And I got tired of waiting for you and went into the living room to sit down, and Pete was there," Dana added. "We've been to almost all the same concerts. Isn't that an amazing coincidence?"

"Amazing," Jessica agreed. She looked at Dana and Pete sitting together and then turned her gaze on Suzanne and Brett. "Stay as long as you want," she told them all, smiling.

They all looked both relieved and embarrassed. "Actually, I should be going," Pete said as he stood up.

Dana stood up, too. "I'll get my stuff later," she told Jessica, her eyes still on Pete.

"I have to run, too," Suzanne said, looking at Brett. "It turns out we're both going to the Altschuler Gallery this afternoon."

With a few more apologies and excuses, the two newly formed couples left the house. Jessica shut the door after them, shaking her head.

"What was that all about?" Elizabeth asked from the top of the stairs.

Jessica chuckled. "It's a long story," she said. She smiled up at her twin. "But it has a happy ending."

Thirteen

On the night of the Valentine's Day dance, Elizabeth spent more time than usual getting dressed. Her new shimmery, blue-green dress looked perfect. The only problem was her hair.

"I just can't get used to it," she told Jessica as she tried clipping back the sides of her curly hair with barrettes.

"Me neither," Jessica agreed in a dry voice.

Elizabeth frowned at her sister's reflection in the mirror. "Does that mean you don't like it?"

"I didn't say that," Jessica said. As she leaned toward the mirror to concentrate on her mascara, one of the straps of her pink dress slipped down her shoulder.

Elizabeth made a face and unclipped the barrettes. So far, her one act of daring spontaneity was a dubious success. It wasn't that her hair didn't look pretty, but she just didn't *feel* like Elizabeth Wakefield.

"It seemed like a good idea at the time," she muttered. "I just wanted to be more adventurous."

Jessica switched her gaze to Elizabeth's face. "Liz, face it. You just aren't the adventurous type."

"Who says?" Elizabeth felt herself growing angry. She pushed her hair back with a headband and stalked into her bedroom. "I could be," she muttered.

She paced back and forth across her pretty blue and cream bedroom. She picked up a pillow and punched it, then tossed it back onto the bed.

I could paint everything bright red, she thought as she frowned at the walls. *That would be a big change.*

The year before, Jessica had painted her whole room brown, completely on the spur of the moment. And even though the entire Wakefield family had made fun of her and referred to her room as the Hershey Bar, it didn't change the fact that Jessica had been willing to take a risk.

"Liz! Todd's here!" Mrs. Wakefield called from downstairs.

Elizabeth grabbed her bag and ran out of her room.

"Hi. You look great!" Todd said as he kissed her hello.

"Thanks," Elizabeth mumbled. She looked up into his eyes. "Todd, you've never said a word about my hair. Do you think I was stupid to perm it?"

Todd blushed. "No," he faltered. "I think it looks—nice."

"You're just saying that," Elizabeth said fondly.

"Well—" He opened the door for her and gave her a sheepish smile. "I liked it the other way better."

Elizabeth sighed and linked her arm with his. They walked out to the car together. "I just want to be more like Jessica."

"What?" Todd stopped in his tracks. "In what way, exactly?"

Elizabeth had to laugh at the nervousness in his voice. Todd had never been overly fond of Jessica. "Just in the way she has of taking chances, trying new things. That's all."

"But you're not like that, Liz," Todd said. "You're so—so comfortable," he decided. He kissed her tenderly. "I love that about you. You make me feel so relaxed."

"Great," Elizabeth said. "I put people to sleep. That's just what I'm talking about."

"That's not what I said, and you know it." Todd started the car. "Come on, let's drop the whole subject. It's sort of dumb, anyway."

It is not *dumb*, Elizabeth wanted to tell him. But she didn't say anything. Privately, however, she was getting worried. If all her friends were so sure she couldn't be spontaneous and adventurous, did that mean they were right? Was she just kidding herself?

When they arrived at school, Elizabeth and Todd found the gymnasium transformed. Big bunches of pink helium balloons were tied everywhere, and red and white streamers curled all over the room. Several couples were already dancing to a slow song.

"Hi, Liz. Hi, Todd," Enid said as she walked up. "Come on over here. We found a table."

A group of their friends was gathered around a big table with a construction paper heart taped in the center. Everyone looked up and said hello when the newcomers appeared.

"I still can't get over your hair, Liz," Olivia Davidson said. "Every time I see you I do a double take."

"Me, too," agreed Sandra Bacon.

Elizabeth touched her hair self-consciously.

But before she could say anything, a familiar voice broke in.

"Liz is trying to be adventurous," Jessica explained, joining the group. Tony Mangino was with her.

"Adventurous?" Robin Wilson said. She laughed. "Liz, you're the one person in this school we depend on to be sane. Don't *you* start doing crazy things."

Everyone else laughed, too. Elizabeth managed a thin smile. "I don't see why it's so hard for you all to believe that I could be adventurous," she said, trying not to sound indignant.

"You're just not the type," Winston Egbert said. "I don't know—I can't picture you doing any of the weird things Jessica's always doing."

Bruce Patman tipped his chair back on two legs. "Leave the adventures to Jessica, Liz," he suggested. He was wearing his usual superior sneer. "Or else who's going to bail *her* out?"

"I don't need to be bailed out, Bruce," Jessica said haughtily. "But thank you for being so concerned."

"You're welcome," he replied.

Todd took Elizabeth's elbow. "Come on, let's dance," he said.

Elizabeth went with Todd out to the dance floor. She didn't say anything, but she was fuming. Everyone seemed to think it was a big joke for her to be more daring and unpredictable. But they were all going to learn not to underestimate her.

Elizabeth Wakefield has a few surprises in her, she thought. *Just wait and see.*

What will Elizabeth do to show her friends she's not so predictable? Find out in Sweet Valley High #63, **THE NEW ELIZABETH.**

Series
Don't miss any of the Caitlin trilogies
Created by Francine Pascal

There has never been a heroine quite like the raven-haired, unforgettable beauty, Caitlin. Dazzling, charming, rich, and very, very clever Caitlin Ryan seems to have everything. Everything, that is, but the promise of lasting love. The three trilogies follow Caitlin from her family life at Ryan Acres, to Highgate Academy, the exclusive boarding school in the posh horse country of Virginia, through college, and on to a glamorous career in journalism in New York City.

Don't miss Caitlin!

MURDER AND MYSTERY STRIKES

SWEET VALLEY HIGH

America's favorite teen series has a hot new line of
Super Thrillers!

It's super excitement, super suspense, and super thrills as Jessica and Elizabeth Wakefield put on their detective caps in the new SWEET VALLEY HIGH SUPER THRILLERS! Follow these two sleuths as they witness a murder...find themselves running from the mob...and uncover the dark secrets of a mysterious woman. SWEET VALLEY HIGH SUPER THRILLERS are guaranteed to keep you on the edge of your seat!

YOU'LL WANT TO READ THEM ALL!

❑ #1: DOUBLE JEOPARDY	26905-4/$2.95
❑ #2: ON THE RUN	27230-6/$2.95
❑ #3: NO PLACE TO HIDE	27554-2/$2.95
❑ #4: DEADLY SUMMER	28010-4/$2.95

HAVE YOU READ THE LATEST!
SWEET VALLEY STARS

❑ #1: LILA'S STORY   28296-4/$2.95

☐	27567	DOUBLE LOVE #1	$2.95
☐	27578	SECRETS #2	$2.95
☐	27669	PLAYING WITH FIRE #3	$2.95
☐	27493	POWER PLAY #4	$2.95
☐	27568	ALL NIGHT LONG #5	$2.95
☐	27741	DANGEROUS LOVE #6	$2.95
☐	27672	DEAR SISTER #7	$2.95
☐	27569	HEARTBREAKER #8	$2.95
☐	27878	RACING HEARTS #9	$2.95
☐	27668	WRONG KIND OF GIRL #10	$2.95
☐	27941	TOO GOOD TO BE TRUE #11	$2.95
☐	27755	WHEN LOVE DIES #12	$2.95
☐	27877	KIDNAPPED #13	$2.95
☐	27939	DECEPTIONS #14	$2.95
☐	27940	PROMISES #15	$2.95
☐	27431	RAGS TO RICHES #16	$2.95
☐	27931	LOVE LETTERS #17	$2.95
☐	27444	HEAD OVER HEELS #18	$2.95
☐	27589	SHOWDOWN #19	$2.95
☐	27454	CRASH LANDING! #20	$2.95
☐	27566	RUNAWAY #21	$2.95
☐	27952	TOO MUCH IN LOVE #22	$2.95
☐	27951	SAY GOODBYE #23	$2.95
☐	27492	MEMORIES #24	$2.95
☐	27944	NOWHERE TO RUN #25	$2.95
☐	26767	HOSTAGE #26	$2.95
☐	27885	LOVESTRUCK #27	$2.95
☐	28087	ALONE IN THE CROWD #28	$2.95

Buy them at your local bookstore or use this page to order.

Bantam Books, Dept. SVH, 414 East Golf Road, Des Plaines, IL 60016

Please send me the items I have checked above. I am enclosing $_____ (please add $2.00 to cover postage and handling). Send check or money order, no cash or C.O.D.s please.

Mr/Ms _____

Address _____

City/State_____ Zip_____

SVH–11/89

Please allow four to six weeks for delivery.
Prices and availability subject to change without notice.

☐	27590	**BITTER RIVALS #29**	$2.95
☐	27558	**JEALOUS LIES #30**	$2.95
☐	27490	**TAKING SIDES #31**	$2.95
☐	27560	**THE NEW JESSICA #32**	$2.95
☐	27491	**STARTING OVER #33**	$2.95
☐	27521	**FORBIDDEN LOVE #34**	$2.95
☐	27666	**OUT OF CONTROL #35**	$2.95
☐	27662	**LAST CHANCE #36**	$2.95
☐	27884	**RUMORS #37**	$2.95
☐	27631	**LEAVING HOME #38**	$2.95
☐	27691	**SECRET ADMIRER #39**	$2.95
☐	27692	**ON THE EDGE #40**	$2.95
☐	27693	**OUTCAST #41**	$2.95
☐	26951	**CAUGHT IN THE MIDDLE #42**	$2.95
☐	27006	**HARD CHOICES #43**	$2.95
☐	27064	**PRETENSES #44**	$2.95
☐	27176	**FAMILY SECRETS #45**	$2.95
☐	27278	**DECISIONS #46**	$2.95
☐	27359	**TROUBLEMAKER #47**	$2.95
☐	27416	**SLAM BOOK FEVER #48**	$2.95
☐	27477	**PLAYING FOR KEEPS #49**	$2.95
☐	27596	**OUT OF REACH #50**	$2.95